Ben Fingered The Tendril Of Hair She Had Tucked Behind Her Ear.

"Your hair. I've identified three of the colors, but this one right here…I'm not quite sure. Burnt sienna, burnt umber, yellow okra—"

"Ochre," Maggie corrected absently.

"Yeah, that's what I said."

For one tingling moment Maggie's world narrowed to include only the man who was standing so close she could see the shards of gold in his whiskey-brown eyes, the iridescent gleam in his crow-black hair.

Without thinking, she reached up and touched his face. He caught her hand and held it against his skin. Heat sizzled between them. Just before he lowered his lips to hers, she heard him whisper, "This is crazy…."

Then there was no more talking, no more thinking, only feeling. And it felt so good, so right in the cool, fragrant morning air. She only wished she were taller so that everything would fit better. It occurred to her that if they were lying down, everything would fit perfectly.

Dear Reader,

Thanks so much for choosing Silhouette Desire—*the* destination for powerful, passionate and provocative love stories. Things start heating up this month with Katherine Garbera's *Sin City Wedding*, the next installment of our DYNASTIES: THE DANFORTHS series. An affair, a secret child, a quickie Las Vegas wedding…and that's just the beginning of this romantic tale.

Also this month we have the marvelous Dixie Browning with her steamy *Driven to Distraction*. Cathleen Galitz brings us another book in the TEXAS CATTLEMAN'S CLUB: THE STOLEN BABY series with *Pretending with the Playboy*. Susan Crosby's BEHIND CLOSED DOORS miniseries continues with the superhot *Private Indiscretions*. And Bronwyn Jameson takes us to Australia in *A Tempting Engagement*.

Finally, welcome the fabulous Roxanne St. Claire to the Silhouette Desire family. We're positive you'll enjoy *Like a Hurricane* and will be wanting the other McGrath brothers' stories. We'll be bringing them to you in the months to come as well as stories from Beverly Barton, Ann Major and *New York Times* bestselling author Lisa Jackson. So keep coming back for more from Silhouette Desire.

More passion to you!

Melissa Jeglinski

Melissa Jeglinski
Senior Editor
Silhouette Desire

Please address questions and book requests to:
Silhouette Reader Service
U.S.: 3010 Walden Ave., P.O. Box 1325, Buffalo, NY 14269
Canadian: P.O. Box 609, Fort Erie, Ont. L2A 5X3

DIXIE BROWNING

Driven to Distraction

Published by Silhouette Books

America's Publisher of Contemporary Romance

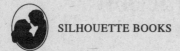 SILHOUETTE BOOKS

ISBN 0-373-76568-1

DRIVEN TO DISTRACTION

Copyright © 2004 by Dixie Browning

Visit Silhouette at www.eHarlequin.com

Printed in U.S.A.

DIXIE BROWNING

is an award-winning painter and writer, mother and grandmother who has written nearly eighty contemporary romances. Dixie and her sister, Mary Williams, also write historical romances as Bronwyn Williams. Contact Dixie at www.dixiebrowning.com, or at P.O. Box 1389, Buxton, NC 27920.

To all the wonderful printmakers whose works
I've collected over the years. (And the artists whose
reproductions I own because I can't afford the originals.)

One

Maggie Riley was nobody's victim. She knew all about situation awareness, having once interviewed a police officer for her column. For the past half hour or so the same dark green pickup truck had been behind her. Traffic had been unusually light all the way from Winston-Salem, but when she'd turned off the interstate onto the state road and the green truck had turned, too—and then it had followed her onto a glorified cowpath that led to her destination—well, she'd started to wonder. Maybe the driver just wanted to tell her that her license plate had fallen off or that a tire was going flat.

On the other hand, he might see her as a potential mugging victim, a woman driving alone. Of course there was always the possibility that he was headed for the same place she was. Peddler's Knob, in the foothills of the Blue Ridge Mountains, site of the Perry Silver Watercolor Workshop. So far as she knew there was no law against artists driving big 4x4 muscle trucks with muddy license plates.

"So enough with the paranoia," she muttered, watching as the dark truck pulled into the small parking lot.

She set the emergency brake and turned her attention to the three-story Victorian house where she would be living and studying for the next six days. A wedding cake of a house, it was riddled with turrets and cupolas, gingerbread and stained glass windows, not to mention a dozen fancy lightning rods.

"Beam me up, Scotty," she murmured.

Two weeks ago when she'd mailed in the application, it had seemed like the perfect solution, even though Maggie knew as much about art as she did nuclear physics. Workshops were for learning, right? So maybe she would actually learn how to paint—not that it was a priority.

Now that it was too late—several hundred dollars too late—second thoughts were swarming thicker than fruitflies at a watermelon bust.

"On your mark, get set—go," she said softly, eyeing the steep, badly graveled path that led to the house where she was scheduled to spend the next six days as an embedded journalist.

She did like the term embedded. It might be stretching it a bit, although she really was here on a covert mission. Never in a million years would she have thought of enrolling in a watercolor workshop if some smooth-talking jerk hadn't targeted her best

friend, who was not only gullible, but rich as chocolate mocha pie.

Leaning over, Maggie tied on her sandals. She
knew better than to try to drive in three-inch platforms
after getting one of them stuck between the brake
pedal and the accelerator the first day she'd worn
them.

With one last glance at the dark green truck again,
she told herself that if the driver had been planning
to do her bodily harm, he would hardly have waited
until there were witnesses. All the same, she waited
to see if he would approach her or drive off in a spray
of gravel, or...

"Holy mackerel, would you look at that," she murmured admiringly. Maggie had enjoyed thinking of
herself as an embedded journalist, out to save her best
friend from being left high and dry with a broken
heart and an empty bank account.

The term embedded took on a whole new concept
as she watched the long, lean figure wearing faded
jeans, western boots and a shirt that barely stretched
across his shoulders as he leaned back inside the cab.
She had yet to see his face but from the waist down,
he looked scrumptious. If this was an example of a
male artist, no wonder Mary Rose had flipped out.
And if this guy turned out to be Perry Silver, she was
licked before she even got started.

Being an advice columnist, Maggie had heard tales
that would curl the hair on a billiard ball. She'd tried
to reason with her friend, to no avail. On the other
hand, if this was the scoundrel in question, she could
almost understand.

Thank goodness she was both experienced and

tough as old boots, because it looked as if she had her work cut out for her. Determination reconfirmed, she got out, stretched and began unloading her luggage, watching from the corner of her eye for the man to turn around so she could see his face. With any luck he'd be ugly as homemade sin.

The picture on the front of the Perry Silver Watercolor Workshop brochure had been of a tall, nice-looking fellow with a toothy smile and a French beret. According to Mary Rose, who had met him at an art exhibit her father had sponsored—the Dilyses were big on corporate sponsorships—he was every woman's dream come true. "Oh, Maggie, he took my hand and held it the longest time, while he stared right into my eyes without saying a word. I felt like the most beautiful woman in the world. Did I tell you his eyes are this brilliant shade of turquoise?" Mary Rose had said when she'd called that evening.

Sure they were. With a little help from Lens-Crafters.

"Oh, I wish you'd been there." Maggie had declined the invitation using the excuse of having a column to write. "We talked and talked, and then when I had to leave to drive Daddy home, Perry took my hand and said I was the reason he'd been drawn to Winston-Salem, because his soul knew there was a kindred spirit waiting for him here."

Maggie had snorted, but covered it with a cough.

"It was like—oh, how can I say it without you thinking I'm crazy? It was like we were lovers in another life and recognized each other instantly. That's the only way I can describe it."

At that point Maggie's gag reflex had threatened.

Using all the tact at her command, she had tried to talk her friend down from cloud nine, but tact had failed and reasoning hadn't made a dent. She'd been about to leave when Mary Rose mentioned endowing a Perry Silver art scholarship at her alma mater. That was when Maggie had realized that quick action was called for.

Oh-oh, tall, dark and dangerous was finally looking her way. Maggie pretended not to be staring as she dragged her big suitcase from the trunk of her dusty hatchback. This job wasn't going to be quite the cinch she'd expected. The man was flat-out gorgeous.

"And you're flat-out dumb as dirt," she muttered as she reached back inside for her art supplies.

Three cars over, the unknown hottie lifted out a small canvas bag and a large plastic shopping bag. Turning her way, he set them on the ground. Maggie caught her breath. Holy mackerel, if this *did* turn out to be Perry Silver it was no wonder Mary Rose had flipped out. He was *better* than handsome—although if her life depended on it, Maggie couldn't have explained what that meant—and words were her business.

"Need another hand?" he called across two sedans and a hardtop convertible. His voice matched his looks. Slow, sweet and gravelly.

"No, thanks," she said airily.

She needed six hands, not three. As usual, she'd packed far too much, but she wasn't about to accept a favor from a stranger, not until she'd had a better chance to size him up. When it came to people, Maggie trusted her instincts, which was why she was here in the first place.

While she was still trying to prioritize the load, he strolled over to join her. "I think you do."

She looked him square in the face, and was sorry she did. The guy flat-out took the breath right out of her lungs, he was that striking. A full head shorter than he was, Maggie managed to look down her nose at him. "I beg your pardon?" Haughty was hard to achieve when you were barely five foot four and a hundred and two pounds only after a big meal. "You're not..."

She started to ask if he were Perry Silver. She knew for a fact that publicity shots were usually heavily retouched, but this man's eyes were the color of clear amber—which also could be due to contact lenses. He was bareheaded, and according to Mary Rose, Perry Silver always wore a beret.

"He wears this beret, and honestly, Mag, he's the most romantic man I've ever seen outside of the movies. Think of a young Gregory Peck. He told me if Raphael had met me first, my portrait would be hanging in the Louvre today. Don't you think that's the sweetest thing you ever heard?"

"Miss?"

"What?" she snapped, jerking her thoughts back in line. He was leaning against her car, staring down into her open trunk, which was half-full of newspapers she kept forgetting to take to the recyclers and other junk she always carried in case of a road emergency. A short length of rope, a flashlight—she reminded herself to check the batteries—and a pair of the world's ugliest shoes.

"Like I said, if you need a hand, I happen to have a free one."

"Then thank you, if you can carry that—" she pointed at her small, tapestry toilet case— "I can handle the rest."

Ignoring her suggestion, he reached for her big suitcase, her computer case and the bundle of art supplies she'd bought at Wal-Mart, leaving her to bring her shoulder bag and her toilet case. She followed him up the hill, studying his lean backside in those jeans that were strategically worn in all the right places.

If he *did* turn out to be Perry Silver, then she might as well give up now and go home. No way could she change any woman's mind about this man, even if she caught him, figuratively speaking, with his hand in the cookie jar.

"Watch the gravel," he warned.

"I'm watching." She tore her gaze from his trim behind and scowled at the rocky, uneven path.

Maggie's idol was Farrah Fawcett, one of the original *Charlie's Angels*. Farrah had never once tripped during the entire series. Maggie knew, as she'd practically memorized the reruns.

Maggie Riley, advice columnist for the *Suburban Record* and investigative journalist-in-training, had tripped a few times. Actually, more than a few times, usually because her attention was elsewhere.

As it was now.

Aside from getting the goods on Perry Silver, she intended to take advantage of the opportunity to learn something about art. The *Suburban Record* didn't have an art critic, but that was not to say they couldn't use one.

Only in her most painfully honest moments did Maggie admit that her "Ask Miss Maggie" column, like the *Record's* few others regular features, served mainly as fillers between ads, school news, meeting announcements and cents-off coupons.

On the other hand, even Woodward and Bernstein had had to start somewhere.

M. Riley, art critic.

Critic of art?

Too self-conscious. She'd settle for art critic.

"This place needs stair steps." He had a dark molasses drawl. Southern, but not Carolina.

"Or an escalator," Maggie said. His legs were roughly a mile longer than hers, even without those slant-heeled cowboy boots. He stopped to wait for her to catch up. "I guess you're here to learn how to paint, too," she ventured. By now she was all but certain he wasn't Perry Silver. Mary Rose would have mentioned more than just his hands and his eyes.

All the same, she introduced herself. "I'm Maggie Riley. I guess we'll be...studying together for the next week."

Several steps ahead of her, he glanced over his shoulder, throwing into relief a profile fit for a Roman coin. "Pleased to meet you, ma'am."

Ma'am? "I didn't catch your name?"

"Ben Hunter. You ready to tackle the last stretch?"

Maggie looked at the last stretch of badly graveled path. "I guess." She was readier for that than she was for her first art lesson. The brochure had described the scenic splendor, which they'd probably be asked to paint. She glanced suspiciously at the misty mountains, the dense forest and the blooming rhododendron. No big deal, she told herself with faux bravado. Splash of blue, splash of green, maybe a streak of pink, and she'd call whatever she created abstract. Who could argue with that? Art was in the eye of the beholder, hadn't somebody famous said that?

Looking ahead, she sized up the group on the porch as she panted up the last few yards. She wasn't particularly surprised to see mostly women. The trouble was, most of them appeared to be middle–aged or older. The only one who looked anywhere near Maggie's age was the blonde in the bandanna bra, but she'd be perfect as bait if Maggie could convince her to cooperate.

It would all work out somehow, she assured herself. She would *make* it work. Mary Rose might be as gullible as a newborn calf, but Maggie wasn't about to be taken in by any smooth-talking leech with turquoise eyes, sensitive hands and a line that would gag an alligator.

Or by a cowboy with whiskey-colored eyes, come to that.

"You okay?" the whiskey-eyed cowboy asked. He paused to wait for her near the rusty wrought iron gate that was half-buried under a jungle of trumpet vine and honeysuckle.

To avoid looking directly at him, Maggie stared up at the house, which appeared to be somewhat shabby up close. "I'm fine," she assured him just as her foot slipped on the gravel.

She staggered, flailed her arms, dropped her toilet kit and managed to regain her balance before tall, dark and devastating could lay a hand on her. When it came to recoveries, she'd had plenty of practice. Graceful, she wasn't.

"It's this darned gravel," she complained. Hopping on her right foot, she ran a finger between her left shoe and her bare foot to dislodge whatever had stuck there.

"Here, let me help," Ben Hunter said, and before she could stop him, he took her foot in his hand and eased a finger between her sole and the platform. "Got it," he said, brushing out a bit of pea gravel.

Clinging to the vine-covered gate for balance, Maggie thought, talk about getting off on the wrong foot!

Before she could catch her breath to thank him, he picked up her bags and set out again, leaving her to follow...or not. She watched as he climbed the steps, strode across to the front door and disappeared inside the house with her luggage.

"Who put a burr under your saddle?" she muttered. He'd been the one to offer his help, she hadn't asked him to grab her ankle and run his hands all over her bare foot.

Nice going, Maggie. You really made a terrific first impression.

Scowling, Ben dumped the bags just inside the door, hooked his thumbs in his hip pockets and waited for his eyes to adjust to the dim interior light. Where the devil had he parked his brain? Now he had to make another trip down the hill to retrieve the gear he'd left on the ground beside his truck.

Silly woman. High heels were one thing—Ben appreciated a sexy shoe and a well-turned ankle as much as the next guy—but a woman who had no better sense than to wear something like that on her feet, well, you had to wonder about her, that's all.

He looked around for whoever was in charge of this tea party. Maybe this hadn't been such a great idea after all. He'd done his share of undercover work—been damned good at it, too. That is, he had until he'd stumbled across evidence that not only were more than half the cops on the force crooked as a corkscrew, the rot went all the way up to the mayor's office—possibly even as far up as Austin. Sick at heart, but not particularly eager to be a dead hero, he'd reported his findings along with documentation to the proper authorities and turned in his badge.

That was when things had started falling apart, including his relationship with the woman he'd been seeing for nearly a year. Not that it had been serious on either side, but they'd been well matched in bed, and Leah hadn't seemed to mind his being a cop.

Then, as if all that weren't enough, he'd had a call from his grandmother, back east. He hadn't seen her in years, but he tried to call a couple of times a month and always wired flowers for her birthday and holidays.

"Benny, I think I might have made a mistake," she'd confided. That's when he'd learned that she'd been bilked out of her savings by some eel posing as an artist who had talked her into "investing" in a bunch of overpriced prints, swearing that within five years they would easily triple in value.

At least, that was Ben's interpretation of what Miss Emma had told him. Personally, he didn't know bad art from good art, but he knew what he liked. What he *didn't* like was any creep who preyed on retirees, especially women. And from what he'd been able to find out, this guy Silver had all the earmarks. In his thirteen-year career as a lawman Ben Hunter had nailed any number of scam artists. He figured that even though he no longer wore a badge, he might as well make it one more for good measure.

He had yet to meet this Silver guy, but he'd studied the picture on the brochure. Big, toothy smile, French headgear, probably to cover a bad comb-over—and a "Trust me" expression.

Oh, yeah, Ben trusted him, all right. About the length of his own shadow, no farther.

There was a string of awards listed on the inside of the three-fold brochure, but who was to say the guy hadn't made them up? The Better Business Bureau didn't have time to check up on every hit-and-run operator.

Standing there in the front hall getting his bearings, his thoughts wandered back to the blonde—not the one with the dark roots and the skimpy red top he'd seen out on the porch, but the other one. Miss Independent in the dumb shoes. Shaggy, dark blond hair, thick, pale lashes and a pair of hazel eyes that kept zapping out messages he interpreted as, "Back off, buddy."

If he was smart, that was a message he'd do well to heed.

Two

If Ben Hunter was an artist, then she had chosen the wrong career, Maggie thought as she signed the roster in the front hall, chose which blanks to fill in and which to leave blank. She picked up her luggage where he'd left it and followed the blonde she had noticed earlier to the room they had both been assigned.

"Oh, my, is this it?"

"Cozy might be an understatement." Suzy James indicated one of three cots in the cramped room off the kitchen. "This one's mine. You might as well take your pick. Whoever we're supposed to share with hasn't shown up yet."

Maggie stacked her luggage beside the cot nearest the small window. Dismayed, she looked around.

"Real bedrooms and bath are on the second floor,

but those rooms are all taken. I must've been one of the last to sign up."

"Me, too," Maggie admitted, wondering if even the best of intentions was worth a week in this claustrophobic environment. *Mary Rose, you owe me, big time.*

While Suzy James perched on the end of her cot and watched, making occasional comments, Maggie unlatched her suitcase and looked for a place to hang the dresses she'd brought.

"Is this your first workshop?"

Warily, Maggie laid aside the flowered sun hat she'd just taken out of her suitcase. The crown had been filled with her underwear. "Um…is that a problem? I'm probably not what you'd call experienced."

"Hey, we're here to learn, right?" Suzy stretched her arms over her head. She had the kind of figure Maggie had given up on achieving when she'd reached her twentieth birthday still wearing a size thirty-two A cup bra—that is, when she wore one at all.

Maggie got out a few packages of the snack food she'd brought along for emergencies and stacked them at one end of the shelf that served as a dressing table. "Help yourself," she offered. "I wasn't sure what to expect, mealwise."

"Sure, thanks. Um…who's your cowboy?"

"My cowboy?"

"Long drink of water with the shoulders and those bedroom eyes. Did y'all come together? I noticed he toted your stuff up the hill."

"We just happened to pull into the parking lot at the same time." Maggie could feel her cheeks growing warm. Her cowboy, indeed. *Don't I wish!* "All I know is he said his name was Ben Hunter."

At least that was all she knew other than the fact that he had a way of moving that could melt the tires on a tractor-trailer. More than once, following him up the path to the house, she had nearly tripped because instead of watching where she was going, she'd been watching the way he moved.

She happened to know he had the kind of voice that resonated in places that sound was not supposed to affect. She also knew she'd do well to keep her mind on her mission and not allow herself to be distracted.

"Have you met Perry Silver yet?" she asked. Seeing no sign of a closet, she folded the dress she'd been holding back into her suitcase. Considering what this week was costing her, was it too much to expect a few coat hangers and maybe a nail or two on the wall?

"Not yet. They say he usually comes in late so he can make this grand entrance."

"Then I guess we'll know when he gets here." Maggie had taken to thinking of him as Perry the Paragon after hearing Mary Rose carry on about everything from the length of his eyelashes to the shape of his fingernails.

Stepping into the adjoining half bath, she set out her toilet articles and then washed her hands. "What now?" she asked, drying off on the towel she'd brought from home.

"We go back out and mingle, I guess. Dibs on the cowboy if you don't want him."

"Help yourself." Maggie had an idea the cowboy

would have something to say about that. Besides, she would much rather Suzy James drew a bead on Perry Silver.

That might have to wait, though. First she needed to explain about Mary Rose and how she was hoping to catch Silver making a play for some other woman, using the same tired old line, so that her friend might wake up before it was too late. Maggie wasn't a meddler, but it was hardly meddling, she rationalized, to expose the truth to spare a friend from future heartbreak.

A dozen or so people had gathered on the deep porch that surrounded three sides of the house. Maggie had intended to join them, but Suzy nodded to the roster where everyone was supposed to sign in and list a few vital statistics. Maggie had put down Clemmons as her hometown and journalist as her occupation. Suzy had listed East Bend and student. Most of the others had put down Retired under occupation.

Ben Hunter had evidently signed in while she'd been unpacking. He'd given Texas as his home address and security as his occupation. "Not real free with details, is he?" Maggie murmured.

"Security," Suzy said thoughtfully. "Wonder what kind of security. Maybe border patrol. He doesn't say where in Texas, but it could be near the border."

"Probably a security guard at a shopping mall," Maggie retorted. She didn't think so, though. He hadn't developed that sexy, loose-limbed walk pounding the terrazzo in some fancy-schmancy shopper's heaven. If she didn't watch out, he was going to prove a major distraction.

"Are you really a journalist?" Suzy indicated Maggie's entry on the roster.

"Well...sort of. That is, I write a weekly column."

"Oh, wow, that must be exciting. Which paper, the *Journal Sentinel*?"

Maggie hated to name the small weekly rag she actually worked for, but she was nothing if not honest. "Just the *Suburban Record* so far. I write the 'Ask Miss Maggie' column." She waited to see if Suzy had ever heard of it. "You wouldn't believe some of the letters I get."

"No kidding? So tell me..." Her voice trailed off as she looked over Maggie's shoulder.

Maggie turned to find herself ensnared by a pair of honey-brown eyes. Ben Hunter said, "I see you're still wearing those shoes."

"I see you're still wearing those cowboy boots. They must have rubber soles, the way you sneak up on people." She closed her eyes and muttered, "Sorry. That was rude."

"It's kind of noisy in here." Evidently he hadn't taken offense. "You might want to wear something a little more sensible when you go outside. Not much level ground around here, and what there is is rocky."

Maggie's eyes flashed a warning. She had heard similar warnings all her life. *Don't climb up on that table, Margaret Lee. Don't run up the stairs! Watch your step, sugar—oops!*

Her entire life had been filled with "oopses," but that didn't mean she was going to change the way she dressed just because some whiskey-eyed cowboy didn't like her style.

Suzy looked from one to the other like a spectator

at a tennis match. "Hey, I'm wearing flip-flops," she said brightly.

Both Ben and Maggie ignored her. Maggie tried to come up with a smart comeback, but before she could think of anything really clever, Ben turned away to join a group of senior citizens.

One of whom, Maggie noticed with interest, wore her pink hair in a single braid along with gold ear hoops, black tights, a peasant blouse and cross-trainers. "Now there," she said softly to Suzy, "is my idea of what an artist should look like."

So saying, she turned, tripped over a pair of big feet and flung out her arms. The elderly gentleman whose feet had been in her way said, "Steady there, little lady."

Smiling weakly, Maggie didn't bother to tell him she was a congenital tripper. Everything from potholes to campaign posters. If she'd heard the words, "Look where you're going" once, she'd heard them a million times. Once she'd even skidded on grains of rice while she was backing up to take a picture and landed on her keester in front of an entire wedding party. Graceful, she wasn't, but after twenty-seven years she had learned to live with her shortcomings.

What was it with women and their crazy shoes? Ben wondered as he edged through the crowd, sizing up the likely candidates for Silver's pitch. He'd seen women dance all night on ice-pick heels and then limp for days. Somebody should've warned her that on anything rougher than a dance floor, stability was more important than style.

On impulse, he worked his way past a gaggle of

gray-heads until he was standing behind her again. Leaning over, he said softly, "You ready to rumble?"

Startled, Maggie Riley spun around. He grinned. "Ready to commit art, that is."

"That's what I came here for," she said defensively.

"Right. Me, too."

The way she looked him over, from the toe of his good-luck boots to the scar on his chin, compliments of a dirtbag armed with a beer bottle, Ben got the idea she was somewhat skeptical about his artistic abilities.

Smart lady. Granted, he was working at a slight disadvantage here, but having once gone undercover with a ring of transvestites who were drugging and robbing businessmen at a restaurateur's convention, he'd considered playing the role of an art student a cinch.

Besides, under the mattress of the room he was sharing with a retired biology teacher was a newly purchased book entitled Watercolor Painting in Ten Easy Lessons. He intended to have at least one of those lessons under his belt by the time the first class was called to order.

"I heard somebody say the maestro's supposed to be here for supper," Suzy James whispered as they found a small table with their names on it a few hours later. "Oh, hell, they've put us right next to the kitchen again. Who do they think I am, Cinderella?"

"At least the food should be hotter." Maggie glanced around the dining room. She made a point of not looking at Ben Hunter, but evidently she wasn't fooling anyone.

Suzy said soulfully, "Is that prime stuff, or what?"

Maggie shrugged. "Good-looking men are always so vain." As if she had firsthand experience. On a scale of one to ten, she was about a four. The best she could hope for was another four—at most, a five.

"So he likes mirrors. I can live with that. I'm not into kinky, understand, but a few mirrors are okay, right?"

Just then there was a stir out in the hall. Both women glanced up expectantly. Suzy whispered, "They say Perry always makes this grand entrance, like, 'Tah-dah, here I am, folks, in all my glory!'"

"You don't sound too impressed. Why'd you sign up for his workshop?"

"Because it was either that or spend another summer working for Daddy in his lumberyard. He's been trying for years to get me interested in taking over the office, but I ask you—a lumberyard?"

"I know what you mean. My father sells insurance and I'm his only offspring. I'm not about to follow in his footsteps, though." Not that he'd ever asked her to.

"I guess not, when you're already a journalist."

"A columnist," Maggie said modestly. Her gaze strayed again to the other side of the dining room, where tall, dark and delicious was frowning. And wouldn't you know it? The man even had a gorgeous frown. Move over, Hugh Jackman. Not for the first time, Maggie told herself that Ben Hunter could easily become a major distraction if she allowed herself to be distracted.

Service was slow. Maggie said, "After seeing the rest of the accommodations I'm surprised we weren't asked to serve ourselves."

"That starts tomorrow. First night's supposed to be special because not everyone gets here in time to pitch in. Didn't you read the fine print in the brochure?"

Maggie had a tendency to skim over fine print. Besides, she'd been too busy studying the picture of Perry the Silver-plated Paragon. "Only enough to know that one week cost an arm and a leg, and you have to bring your own art supplies and linens."

A grim-faced woman slapped two cups of coffee onto the table. Maggie had wanted iced tea, but she wasn't about to make waves, not on the first night.

Suzy murmured, "Judging from the stir out in the hall, I think you-know-who's about to make his entrance. If you've never seen him before, don't be taken in by his looks."

"You've met him?"

"He came to our house once last spring trying to get my father to donate a prize."

"A prize for what?"

"You know—different businesses donate prize money for the advertising. The more prizes, the more entries—the more entries, the more entry fees are collected and the more our guy Perry takes home after expenses. He's a genius when it comes to boosting sponsors."

Which was precisely how he had come to meet Mary Rose, Maggie reminded herself. "Sounds like you're not exactly his biggest fan. You sure you wouldn't rather work for your father?"

"No way. I give him two weeks every summer while his secretary goes to Myrtle Beach, but that's it. You don't meet guys like Texas in a lumberyard office." She nodded toward the table where Ben Hunter was seated and smacked her lips. "I wonder what he's doing here."

"Same thing we are. Trying to learn how to paint."

"Uh-uh. I bet he's ATF. I've heard there's still some white liquor being produced around here."

"Alcohol, tobacco and firearms? How is studying art supposed to help him locate a hidden still?" Maggie sipped her coffee. It was cold and weak.

"Who knows? Maybe he just needed an excuse to hang around in the area. There's nothing much around these parts but this place, and you know what? I wouldn't be surprised if whoever built the place back in the twenties made his fortune in moonshine whiskey." Elbows on the table, Suzy was getting into the conspiracy thing.

"Maybe, but who makes the stuff anymore when you can buy whiskey in any ABC store?"

"White lightning, my de-ah, is an acquired taste. Once you've acquired it, Jack Daniel's pales by comparison."

Maggie hooted with laughter. From the corner of her eye she saw Ben Hunter turn and look her way. Feeling her cheeks burn, she studiously applied herself to the stewed chicken and overcooked vegetables.

"Don't look now, but here comes the maestro now," Suzy whispered a few minutes later. "I've heard he makes the rounds introducing himself, so smile and be sweet. You might even get a passing grade."

Maggie looked up into a pair of turquoise eyes that had to be—simply had to be—contacts. God didn't make eyes like that.

"Ah, we meet again, Miss James." Perry Silver smiled at Suzy, then turned to Maggie. "Let me guess. This would be Miss Riley, right? Margaret L. Riley, the journalist? I'm honored, my dear. May I join you for a few minutes?"

From the far side of the dining room, Ben frowned as he watched Silver make his way across the room to the table by the kitchen door. The slick jackass was hanging all over the Riley woman, ignoring the bleached blonde.

Conversation continued around him. One of the women said, "I remember thinking at the time that ten thousand was a fortune. Nowadays it wouldn't even last six months, not at today's prices."

"What? Oh, right," someone else said. "GI Insurance."

Ben had been gently sounding out his dinner partners, trying to squeeze in a subtle hint about a few of the scams that targeted senior citizens. New ones cropped up every day, and for any seniors who went online, the dangers tripled. On his left sat Janie Burger, whose husband, a World War II veteran, had died a couple of years ago, leaving her with an eighty-six Plymouth van, a house in need of reroofing and a ten-thousand dollar GI life insurance policy. Her daughter had treated her to Silver's workshop in order to—as Janie put it—haul her up from the slough of despond, which Ben interpreted as depression. Although the lady didn't strike him as depressed. Far from it.

"I'll certainly never get rich as an artist," she said with a self-deprecating chuckle, "but at least I won't have to worry about buying Christmas gifts this year. They'll all get bad watercolors and won't have the nerve to tell me what they think of my talent. Works every time."

Pulling his attention away from the table by the kitchen door, Ben made an ambiguous, hopefully appropriate comment. He admired the lady's spunk, as well as her unlikely pink hair.

"We're supposed to be intermediates, aren't we? Didn't it say so on the brochure?" That from Charlie Spainhour. The two men had been assigned a room together. "I took a few courses some years back, but haven't done any painting since my late wife decided the bathroom needed a pink ceiling."

Ben glanced again at the table by the kitchen door, where little Ms. Riley was smirking up at Silver, batting her eyelashes like she'd caught a cinder and was trying to dislodge it. If she wanted to play teacher's pet, it was no skin off his nose. Hell, she wasn't even all that pretty.

The conversation eddied around him while he watched the Riley woman's reaction to whatever Silver was saying. Lapping it up with a spoon. He shook his head and forced his attention back to his own dinner companions.

Charlie said, "I don't know if it'll come back to me or not. Like I said, it's been a while."

"Don't worry, if he's as good a teacher as I've heard he is, he'll fill in the gaps," said the white-haired woman at the end of the table—Georgia something or other. "By the end of the week we'll all be intermediates—some of us already are. I guess you can fake it that long.''

Evidently, Ben was the only one present who had never tried his hand at painting before. He was beginning to feel more than ever like a fish out of water.

Janie, Ben's favorite so far, removed her red-framed bifocals and cleaned them with a napkin as her eyes crinkled in another smile. "Frankly, my dear, I don't give a darn. I painted my first bad watercolor before that boy was even out of diapers. Been painting them ever since.''

It garnered a few chuckles, including Ben's. Not that it was all that funny, but who knew better than an undercover specialist how to fit in? So far it looked like a pretty decent group, ready to lighten up for a week instead of sitting home watching their IRAs bottom out while they waited for the monthly social security stipend. Maybe he should have brought Miss Emma along. So far as he knew, the only thing she'd ever painted was her kitchen chairs, but who was to say she wouldn't discover a latent talent?

The desultory conversation continued with only an occasional comment from Ben. It turned out that Georgia and Janie were friends; both widows, both retired teachers. Janie and Charlie had met before, evidently having taught at the same school.

Placing his silverware on his plate, Ben angled his chair slightly for a better view of the other diners. He was beginning to see a pattern in the enrollment. Retirees took precedence, with just enough variety, such as himself and the pair across the room, to throw off suspicion.

On the get-acquainted roster on the hall table, more

than half the enrollees had listed Retired under occupation. Ben had put down Security, which wasn't
actually a lie. Not that he couldn't lie with the best
of them when the occasion demanded, but he preferred not to. Less to trip over.

He glanced over at the Riley woman again. She
had dressed for the occasion in a long button-front
dress with a matching scarf. He couldn't see her feet,
but no doubt she was still wearing those same dumb
platforms with the loop around her big toe, in spite
of his good advice.

At the moment, she was fussing about something.
Now why did that not surprise him? He didn't know
much about her disposition, but it hadn't taken him
long to learn that she bristled with attitude. In a guy,
he'd heard it referred to as a Napoleon complex—not
necessarily a bad thing, depending on how it was
used. It could turn a guy into an overachiever or make
him a real pain.

Where Riley was concerned, he had a feeling it
might be the latter.

With one last long look at her profile—short,
straight nose, well-defined jaw, a tempting speck of a
mole and full lips that at the moment were clamped
tighter than a—

Yeah, well…he was going to have to watch his
similes, too. This place was filled with respectable
grannies. His own had peeled the bark off him when
he'd forgotten and let slip a few choice words the
other day when a damn-fool driver nearly shaved the
paint off his front fender by cutting in front of him
on the way to the grocery store.

He might not be able to recover Miss Emma's

losses, but he could make damn sure the same thing didn't happen to anyone else's granny. Not on his watch.

"Our resident genius seems mighty interested in that table over by the kitchen," Charlie, high school biology teacher, murmured. He nodded toward where Silver was still hanging over the two younger women. The platinum blonde with the dark roots had tossed on a white shirt over the red bra, but hadn't bothered to button it up.

It was the other one that held Ben's attention. Maggie Riley. According to the roster, she was from Clemmons which, if memory served, was less than a half hour's drive from where his grandmother lived in Mocksville. Under occupation, she'd written journalist. Interesting, he mused.

None of your business, he reminded himself firmly. She could be a nuclear scientist and it still wouldn't matter. It was the blue-haired ladies, including Janie, whose shoulder-length hair just happened to be pink, who were his real targets. Those were the ones Silver would go for if Ben's predictions proved accurate. If he could wise them up in time, they could go forth and spread the word any way they chose to. Senior citizens' groups, newsletters—whatever. This was at best a borderline case of fraud, but for individuals on fixed incomes, it could be devastating.

"What? Oh, yeah—I'll take natural hair over nylon any day," he said as if he knew what the devil they were talking about. He figured at least half the women here weren't wearing the hair color they were born with. Wigs or not, Georgia, with her white brush cut, and Riley with the attitude and the shaggy, straw-colored hair were probably among the very few who were wearing their natural color.

"Some like a flat, but me, I prefer round."

It took him a moment, but he got it. They were talking about brushes, not wigs. He had one. Didn't remember if it was flat or round, as it came with the set of paints he'd bought. He figured as long as you wet it, rubbed it on the paint and wiped it across the paper, one shape was as good as another.

Although rice pudding was about six yards down on his list of favorites, he lingered over dessert while the others went out to watch the sunset. Technically, the sun had set about half an hour ago, but according to Janie, there was something special about the last rays of color that shot up from behind the mountains.

When he saw the two at the back table rake back their chairs, he collected his dishes, stacked them with the others on the table, and headed toward the kitchen. The lady in the kitchen looked as if she could use a hand, and his were available. And if it happened to take him within a couple of feet of Ms. Riley and her haystack hair, so be it.

She glanced up when he passed by with his hands full of dishes. "Oh, are we supposed to do that?" Rising, she started gathering up the dishes on her table.

Suzy looked from Ben to Maggie and lifted a brow. "See you later, okay?" she said with what could only be called a smirk.

Riley followed him out to the kitchen, where the cook was elbow deep in suds. Evidently, the place didn't run to a dishwasher, mechanical or otherwise.

"Here's these," he said.

Without glancing around, the woman said, "Scrape
'em in the can, leave 'em on the counter."

Ben looked at Maggie. Maggie looked at Ben.
That's when he noticed that her eyes had almost as
many different shades as her hair. By tomorrow, he
might even be able to name a few, but for now he'd
have to settle for brown, yellow and blue-green. The
eyes, not the hair.

"What, do I have dirt on my face?" The multi-
colored eyes flashed a warning.

He forced himself to look away. "Sorry—just
thinking about tomorrow."

"Oh. Well, sure. Me, too. That is, I'm really looking forward to, uh—wetting some paper."

"Gimme them cups," the woman at the sink said,
and they both reached for the thick white cups they'd
just placed on the counter. Ben's arm struck Maggie's
hand, which struck the stack of cups. They watched
them bounce on the sagging linoleum floor. Fortunately, only one broke. They were the thick, white
institutional kind.

"Sorry," he said. Quickly, he rounded up the un-
broken cups while Maggie ripped off a handful of
paper towels and moped up a splash of coffee. They
ended up kneeling head to head, and he caught a faint
whiff of apples and something else—maybe coco-
nut—that hadn't been on the menu tonight.

And neither is she, he reminded himself.

Fleeing before they could do any more damage,
neither of them waited for the thanks that probably
wouldn't be forthcoming anyway, judging from the
way the woman was scowling. Maggie said, "Oops."

Ben said, "Yeah," and grinned.

The others were beginning to straggle inside after watching the sunset. Janie with the pink hair was guffawing. She had a great laugh, apparently oblivious to the fact that her face crinkled up like used wrapping tissue. She probably had better sense than to invest in any of Silver's junk anyway, but Ben would watch over her, just in case. He liked her.

Her friend Georgia, too. Ben sized her up as a likely candidate. White hair, flowered dress, embroidered button-front sweater, support hose and cross trainers. Not to mention a rock the size of a golf ball on her third finger, left hand. With her swollen knuckles, she probably couldn't get it off, poor woman. He'd keep a special eye out for her. First time he caught Silver spending an unusual amount of time with her, he'd follow up with a word of caution.

Okay, Janie and Georgia and who else? There were at least a dozen candidates, not counting the two blondes and the two guys, including Charlie and himself.

Maybe he should hold an impromptu seminar on how not to be drawn into a sucker's trap. He had yet to work out a plan for getting the goods on Silver, but he was used to going in without an ironclad plan. A good cop left plenty of maneuvering room; he'd learned that his first year on the job when he'd walked in on a convenience store robbery and got a face full of Reddi-wip. Since then he'd at least had sense enough to work the perp around to the bagged goods before trying to cuff him. A face full of corn chips couldn't do a whole lot of damage.

"Wanna join the others out on the porch?" he asked.

Riley looked at him a full thirty seconds before shaking her head. "No thanks," she said, and walked off.

Nice going, Hunter. From now on, keep your mind on the job you're supposed to be doing.

Three

It was a good hour earlier than her usual bedtime when Maggie headed for her assigned quarters. Beginning tomorrow the students would be responsible for meals. They were to work out a plan among themselves. Suzy, seated in the middle of her cot, was painting her toenails. She suggested that some of the older women would naturally want to take charge.

"Why?"

"Well…because, I mean, most of them have been married, so they're used to cooking."

So was Maggie, not that she intended to advertise it. Her mother had left home when Maggie was eleven, after announcing that life was a fleeting thing. Several weeks later she'd written from a commune out in Idaho, something about being free to become herself. She still came home occasionally, never staying more than a few days. Actually, she hadn't been home in several years, but at least she still wrote when she remembered to. Handmade postcards for the most part, filled with colored drawings of moons and stars and rainbows and elves.

So maybe, Maggie mused, she had inherited some artistic talent after all.

She considered unpacking her laptop to record a few first impressions to work into a special column once the week was over. With any luck, her editor might accept it—might even spring for a small bonus. If she earned enough to pay income taxes she could write off this whole horribly expensive week as research—but first she would have to write about it.

She found a place to set up her laptop by shifting Suzy's array of cosmetics, then looked around for an outlet within reach. Her batteries were probably dead. Since she rarely used them, she rarely remembered to check them. Why didn't someone invent a computer that plugged into a cell phone? Or maybe they already had. Technology wasn't her thing, but that would bear checking out.

She might even get a column about that, too. Technology for the technophobe. Not that she was really phobic, she was simply too busy to keep up with the stuff.

"I still don't think he's an artist," Suzy announced out of the blue.

"Who?" As if she didn't know. "All the famous artists have been men." Maggie continued checking the pockets of her computer case to see if she'd brought along any batteries. If so, they were too old to have any juice left in them.

"They say that about chefs, too, but what about Julia Child?"

"What about that Western artist, whatsisname?"

"You're asking me?" Suzy was using Crayolas to hold her toes apart to keep the polish from smearing.

"You know who I mean—he's named something to do with guns. Colt? Browning? Oh, yeah—Remington."

"He probably carries one. A gun, I mean. He said he was in security." Carefully, Suzy began pulling out the Crayolas. "Man, I wouldn't mind a taste of that kind of security."

"Maybe he's a model," Maggie suggested.

"In that case, I'm devoting the rest of my life to art."

Maggie said, "How did we get off on this subject, anyway?" As if she didn't know. "I need to take some notes in case I want to write about it."

"Okay, first note—your heroine's name is Suzy and your hero's name is Ben. Is that a virile name, or what?"

Maggie threw a small instruction leaflet, which she'd never bothered to read, across the room. It landed among the shoes near the bed. Four pairs of Suzy's, one pair of hers.

"I'm going to grab a shower while everybody's still out on the porch." Collecting soap, shampoo and a loose cotton shift that doubled as a robe, Maggie headed upstairs where one of the larger rooms had been turned into a communal bathroom. There was a single claw-foot tub, three lavatories, three commodes and three shower stalls. The men evidently had a tiny bathroom down the hall, which was a rough indication of the usual ratio between men and women.

Lathering her hair, she wondered if Silver culled through the applicants, deliberately choosing the ones he wanted to include. Using what criterion, she wondered. She hadn't been particularly surprised to see so few men. The surprising thing had been that so many of the women were over fifty. It only solidified her suspicion that he was far more interested in money than in sex or romance.

On the other hand, he'd been hanging all over Suzy at supper tonight. At this point Suzy was more interested in Ben Hunter, but maybe that didn't mean she wouldn't cooperate for the good of the mission. Lumber money was as good as pickle money, especially when the only heir just happened to be an attractive daughter of marriageable age.

It never occurred to Maggie to consider herself a candidate. Her father sold insurance. He didn't own the company—didn't even manage the three-man agency, which was one of the reasons Maggie had attended a community college instead of university; why she'd gone to work for a pittance at the *Suburban Record* until she could get a real job at the *Twin-City Journal*. Even in state tuition cost a fortune, and besides, her father needed her at home. Left to himself he'd have ended up eating bacon and eggs and real butter and drinking four-percent milk in spite of knowing better.

Before her mother had left they'd dined more often than not on things like tofu, tahini and soybeans in one form or another. Maggie had joined her father in pigging out on junk food between meals, but now that she was older she had settled on a more moderate path. Whole-grain, low-fat, with lots of fresh fruit and vegetables. If she occasionally backslid when she was away from home, that was nobody's business but her own. As long as she had only one functional parent, she fully intended to keep him that way. Let her mother go on drifting from one mushroom field to another, playing her zither, smoking pot and remembering every six months or so that she still had a family back east. Fortunately, Maggie had inherited a broad streak of practicality from her father, enough to take care of him and anyone else who needed it.

"Any hot water left?" Suzy was in the room when Maggie got back from her shower.

"Gobs. Look, I need you to do me a favor." And so she explained about Mary Rose and why she was really here.

"Geez, I don't know, Riley." Leaning back on her elbows, Suzy admired her colorful toenails. "I sort of had my eye on the cowboy. Besides, Perry spent most of his time with that lady with the buzz cut and the three-carat diamond."

"Georgia, I think her name is." Maggie sat on the room's only chair, which lacked a back and could more properly be termed a stool. She toweled her hair. "The cowboy will wait. All I need is one good example of Perry reeling out the same old line he used on Mary Rose, and I'll have him dead to rights."

"Would she believe you?"

"If I could get it on tape, it would be even better." Maggie waited hopefully for Suzy to offer her body to be wired. When no such offer was forthcoming,

she shrugged and said, "She knows I never lie...
unless it's absolutely necessary."

"If I get the goods on Silver, do I get dibs on the
cowboy?"

"Unless he's married or otherwise out of the running, he's all yours," Maggie said magnanimously,
as if it were up to her. If she had anything to say
about it, she might not be so generous.

"He's not wearing a ring." Suzy went through a
few lethargic yoga movements. "There's my day's
exercise. I'm a firm believer in moderation in all
things."

Maggie continued to towel her hair, her mind on
the man who kept popping into her thoughts like a
sexy poltergeist. "He's probably not going to model,
since he signed the register like all the rest of us."

"Besides, if he were a model, he'd be busy trying
on jockstraps."

"Perish the thought," Maggie said, grinning.

"I don't want to perish the thought, it's too tempting."

"About tomorrow—" Maggie was determined not
to lose sight of her mission. "We're all going to have
to paint something. How good are you?"

Suzy shrugged. "It's been a while."

"I've never even tried to draw anything since I
used to do stuff in school, mostly stick figures standing under a rainbow."

"What do you bet we're not the only amateurs
here?"

"Um-hmm..." Maggie was having trouble picturing Ben Hunter as an artist, although she couldn't
have said quite why. Maybe because of his boots. Or

maybe those powerful arms. She'd be willing to bet those strong hands and muscular forearms had done more than wield a paintbrush.

"But then, hey—if it weren't for us amateurs, Perry would be out of a job, right?" Suzy said brightly.

After that, they talked about clothes—whether or not they'd brought the right kind—and boyfriends. Suzy was currently juggling three; Maggie didn't have time for even one, although she had her eye on a young high school coach.

By the time the new roommate, Ann Ehringhaus, showed up, Maggie was already yawning. After introductions all around, Suzy pointed out the amenities, such as they were. When Ann sneezed for the third time, Maggie murmured something about allergies. While the other two women talked softly, Maggie fell asleep and dreamed of a Ben Hunter who segued into one of those famous male statues wearing a fig leaf and a strategically draped shawl, with a quiver full of watercolor brushes on his back. He was leering at her.

Mercy! No wonder she woke up even before the alarm went off with the mother of all headaches.

Leaving the other two women still sleeping, Maggie dressed quietly and tiptoed into the kitchen, following the beguiling aroma of freshly brewed coffee. When a shaft of sunlight slanting through the window struck her, she winced and shut her eyes.

"Not a morning person, hmm?"

Her stomach did a funny little lurch and she blinked at the figure silhouetted against the open back door. Wouldn't you know the first person she'd see before she could even wash down a handful of pills would be Apollo in person. If he'd been wearing a fig leaf and shawl, she'd have run screaming off down the hill.

Instead he was wearing the same faded jeans he'd worn yesterday, which were as good as a roadmap pointing out strategic points of interest. Her good-morning sounded more like the snarl of a pit bull.

"It's probably the altitude," he told her solicitously.

She shot him a suspicious look, and he said, "Headache, right? Flying does it to me, even in a pressurized cabin. We're not all that high here, but—"

"Thanks, I don't need a diagnosis," she growled. "Lack of sleep always gives me a headache." With any luck, it would be gone before the first class started—and so would he.

"Me, I slept like a log."

She shot him a saccharine smile. "Goody for you."

"We're on our own from now on." Reaching inside a cabinet, he took out a box of sweetened cereal and frowned at the picture of tiny, pastel-colored shapes.

Maggie had brought her own cereal. It was whole grain and probably not as tasty as the one he was holding. His arms and his hands were tanned. There was no lighter circle on his third finger, left hand, to indicate he had recently worn a ring.

He said, "I checked the refrigerator. The kitchen's stocked with basics, but they're pretty, ah—basic. Eggs, bacon. Bunch of green stuff."

"Do you have to talk so much?" She winced as she crossed through the patch of sunlight again.

"Reckon not. Reckon we could just dance."

She goggled at him. No other word to describe it. She did her best to blot out the memory of the impressive creature with his undraped loins and his quiver of brushes, that had haunted her early morning dreams. The image was already losing the sharp edges, but she could still see those muscular calves and the flat, ridged abdomen where the shawl draped low on one hip before swinging up to his shoulder.

"If you don't mind," she said haughtily, "I'd rather not talk before I've had my morning pint."

"Yes, ma'am. Better warn you, though—it's pretty strong. You might want to water it down some. Be somebody along pretty soon to start the bacon and eggs."

She mimicked talking with her fingers. He looked suitably chastened and covered his mouth with his hand. And darn it, he really did have gorgeous hands. Maggie wasn't entirely certain what an artistic hand was supposed to look like, but artistic or not, his long, square-tipped fingers were perfectly proportioned for the square palm.

And if she'd ever even considered a man's hands in that respect, she had to be plum out of her mind. What the devil was happening to her normally sharp-as-a-tack brain? She was here on a mission. She didn't have time for this kind of distraction.

She poured herself a mug of coffee and by the time she turned around, Ben had placed a jug of whole milk and a can of evaporated on the table, along with a sugar bowl, a jar of honey and a stack of pink pack-

ets of sweetener. He grinned as if he'd offered her
the crown jewels.

"Thank you," she croaked. Croaked because her
voice was always rusty first thing in the morning. She
was used to seeing her father off to work in silence
and taking her pint of coffee into the ex-utility room
she laughingly called her office, where she worked on
her column until noon. If any calls came in, she let
the machine take them.

"Really," she said when he continued to look at
her as if she were something he'd found under a microscope. Or under a rock.

"Look, you're a nice man and I'm a grungy cur-
mudgeon. I'm sorry, but that's just the way it is,
okay?"

Bemused was the only word she could think of to
describe the way he looked at her. As if whatever it
was he'd discovered under the microscope—or the
rock—had suddenly launched into a full orchestra
rendition of the "Star Spangled Banner." She sometimes had that effect on men. They didn't know what
to make of her, and so mostly, they made nothing.
Which suited her just fine, it really did. It always had.

Until just recently…

Without a word, Ben Hunter eased up from the
spoke-backed kitchen chair, tipped her a nod and let
himself out onto the side porch. A few moments later
she could hear the creak of the swing.

Darn it, why did she do that? She knew all about
women who were their own worst enemy. So certain
men wouldn't like them that they went out of their
way to prove they didn't care. She'd written about

that kind of behavior. The thing was, she'd never before realized she followed the pattern.

As the first class began to take shape, each of the
several long tables filled, some with three students, a
few with four. Maggie, Suzy and the latecomer, Ann
Ehringhaus, chose a smaller table near the back of the
studio. Without intending to, Maggie looked around
for Ben and found him setting up several tables away
with two women and a guy who looked like G. Gor-
don Liddy—same bald head, same beetle brows, but
a smaller mustache.

There were no easels. There were also no chairs.
Suzy muttered something about a half-ass operation.
Ann sneezed. Maggie shifted restlessly and considered giving up on this whole crazy idea. What had
started as a simple rescue mission and expanded to a
story op—M. L. Riley, embedded somewhere in the
foothills of the Blue Ridge Mountains—was looking
more like an expensive mistake.

Hardly her first. She simply hadn't thought things
through, and now she was about to be exposed as the
fraud she really was. She could no more paint a picture than she could hop on a broomstick and fly. What
on earth had made her believe she could pull it off?

From somewhere off-stage, music started up,
screeched to a halt and then started again. To the
strains of something vaguely Celtic, vaguely New
Age, Perry made his grand entrance, scattering smiles
all around. He was wearing his trademark beret, even
though the temperature was already in the mid-
seventies and the old house evidently didn't run to air
conditioning. He took his place at a table in front that

had been set up with a child's plastic beach pail filled
with water, a big, smeary palate, an enormous sheet
of paper on a drawing board and an alabaster vase
filled with at least a dozen brushes of all sizes and
shapes.

"So that's what all the plastic pails are for," Maggie murmured indicating the yellow one beside her
stack of stuff.

"You'll have to fill and empty your own. Perry's
the only one who gets serviced," Ann whispered.

"Now," the tall, willowy artist said, his mellifluous voice blending with the music, "I'll start off with
a demonstration and then you'll all have half an hour
to do your version of what I've painted. We want
quick and sloppy today. This is just a loosening-up
exercise. By the way, how many of you can still touch
your toes?"

Maggie looked at Suzy, who shrugged. For the first
time since she'd arrived the night before, Ann smiled.
"Wait, you'll see," she whispered.

Across the room, Ben wondered what the hell the
guy meant by that question. And what was with all
the flutes and harps? To cover up the groans from
people who hadn't touched their toes in decades? Hell
yes, he could touch his toes. He might be on the shady
side of thirty, but he could still take down a cream
puff like Silver with one hand tied behind him.

Only this time he was going to do it nice and legal.
Scare the hell out of him so that nobody's gullible
granny would get taken for a ride on Hi-Ho Silver.

Bracing his feet apart, Ben crossed his arms over
his chest and waited for the show to begin. Beside
him, Janie Burger planted her hands on her hips and

did the same. Georgia said something about not enough liniment in the world to make her try it, and Charlie chuckled.

Meanwhile, in the front of the room, Perry Silver had already started on the morning's masterpiece, working flat on the table. From time to time he pursed his lips, stepped back, tilted his head and muttered an unintelligible incantation, after which, while his audience tried vainly to see what he was doing, he would lunge forward to add another touch. Gradually a streak of muddy color appeared on the floor where he repeatedly slung wet paint from his brush.

"No wonder the floors in here look like sh—like sugar," Ben muttered. "Why the devil doesn't he hold the thing up so we can see what the—so we can see what he's doing?" Out of respect for his associates, he was trying to cull the profanity from his vocabulary, but it wasn't easy.

"With watercolor, mostly you do it flat so you can tilt it whatever way you want the paint to flow," Janie whispered.

"Oh. Right." Going undercover as an artist might not be the swiftest idea he'd ever had.

Georgia nudged him and whispered, "Did the brochure say anything about having to pass a physical first?"

With a slow smile, Ben shook his head. The lady with the white buzz cut smelled like his granny. Combination of almond-scented hand lotion and arthritis-strength liniment. It reminded him of why he was here.

Silver glanced up with a boyish grin and said, "I know, I know, it seems like forever, but this little bit over here just simply isn't working. Give me another minute, dears, all right?''

Dears?

There was a general shuffling of tired feet. Someone sneezed—the latecomer with the allergies, probably.

Someone snickered. Had to be Maggie. He glanced around, and sure enough, her hand was covering her mouth and her eyes were alight with mischief. Today she was wearing a sleeveless blue chambray thing with what looked like a man's undershirt underneath. On her, it looked just fine.

Ben winked at her. Last time he remembered winking at a woman he'd been about fifteen, all beered up and looking for action.

Found it, too, if memory served.

God, he'd had some narrow escapes. This just might turn out to be one more in a long list, unless he could keep his mind on his mission.

''You're at the wrong table, hon,'' Janie whispered. Her pastel-colored hair was held back this morning with a twisted scarf. She was wearing black tights again along with a baggy pink sweatshirt sporting a risqué slogan. It occurred to him that maybe no one had told her she was pushing seventy.

You go, lady, he encouraged silently.

''Did you say something, Miss…Riley, isn't it?'' The maestro looked up, light from the north-facing windows emphasizing the bags under his eyes. Ben figured the picture on the cover of the brochure had been either heavily retouched or taken quite a few years earlier.

"Sorry. I was just—just eager to see what you've done."

Bless her heart, she was lying through her pearly whites. Ben winked again. It had to be a twitch. Maybe an ingrown eyelash.

Then Silver whipped out a hair dryer, switched it on and waved it over whatever he'd just done. Probably another "investment" like those Miss Emma had paid a whole slew of social security money for. If there was any way he could squeeze a refund out of this cheesy bastard he intended to do it.

"Oh, my, he's done it again," murmured Georgia as Perry propped his drawing board up on the easel so that it faced the class. She applauded. A few others picked it up, but Silver waved his hand and the applause quickly faded.

"Now, using my feeble attempt as an example, let's all see what we can come up with. Quickly, quickly—let the medium know who's boss."

Let the medium know who was boss? What the hell was *that* supposed to mean? Ben glanced over his shoulder and happened to catch Maggie's eye. She shrugged. He shook his head. At least this time they were in agreement. A regular meeting of the minds. He could think of several other areas where he wouldn't mind meeting her.

"You have thirty minutes," Silver said. "Impressions only, we'll get to details later in the week."

Charlie, on the far end of Ben's table, asked if there were any chairs. Perry lifted his eyebrows, but Charlie, a high school biology teacher a year away from retirement, was not intimidated. "In my classroom I stand,'' he stated. "On vacation, I sit unless I've got a golf club in my hand.''

Ben wondered what the hell the older man was doing here when he could be outside in the fresh air beating the stuffing out of a little white ball?

"Is anyone else unable to stand for more than fifteen minutes? If so, you might want to consider dropping out now.'' Adjusting his beret, the instructor surveyed the room as if daring anyone to take the challenge.

"Do I get a refund if I drop out?'' Charlie asked.

"I believe the terms were clearly stated in your application.''

"I guess that means no.''

Sounds of disapproval moved through the room on the pollen-laden breeze, drawing a variety of responses. Janie uncovered what she called a watercolor block—a stack of rough pages glued together on the edges. She leaned past Ben to smile at Charlie.

Ignoring a few murmurs of discontent, Silver pointed out first one area and then another in his landscape, over which he had quickly taped a white mat, as if to lend it legitimacy. "Note the contrasts,'' he instructed. "Dark against light, light against dark.''

Hard to get one without the other, Ben thought, but then he wasn't feeling particularly charitable.

"Gradation, there's your sense of depth. Note the sharpest areas—in other words, the greatest contrast—falls near the center of interest, while everything else seems to soften. Blended washes. Do we see this?''

"With or without my trifocals?'' someone asked, to the accompaniment of a few snickers.

And then, Lord bless her, Maggie spoke up. "Which part wasn't working…sir? If you don't mind my asking."

Janie bit her lip. Charlie said something about his feet not working, plus a few other parts he could mention, but wouldn't. Georgia dipped a brush that could easily be used for window trim into her plastic pail and dragged it over a pan of colors that looked as if it had been caught in the middle of a paint war.

By the time they broke for a glass of sweetened iced tea, everyone had committed their thirty minutes' worth of art. Ben had done his share of cursing, but fell silent after the first remonstrative look from Georgia. "Sorry," he said. "I'm trying to break the habit, but the damn paper—darned paper keeps puckering."

Charlie offered a few euphemisms, several of which were biological terms which, translated to street parlance, wouldn't pass muster. Janie called him a dirty old man, but grinned when she said it. She handed Ben a couple of clothespins and showed him how to use them to control the swelling of wet paper. All three of his tablemates commented freely, the comments for the most part flying over Ben's head.

Washes, bleeds, drybrush? Hell, he couldn't even manage the lingo. How the devil was he supposed to learn how to paint a picture?

Answer? He wasn't. No point in getting too caught up in the action. That wasn't why he was here.

He added a long squiggle of red across his mountain just because he'd always liked the color. It turned brown. "Well, shi—ucks," he grumbled. "I know damned well I dipped my brush in red."

Janie laughed and pointed out that mixed together, the colors he'd used make mud.

And then Maggie was there, peering over his shoulder to see how badly he'd embarrassed himself. He felt like covering it up, but he had too damn much pride.

"Oh, wow," she breathed reverently. "You're almost as good as I am. Does either of us really need to be here?"

"I'm seriously startin' to wonder," Ben growled.

Maggie felt like patting him on the head—or maybe somewhere more accessible. It made her feel better about her own charade to know that she and Suzy weren't the only two in the room without a clue. Mr. Spainhour wasn't bad, and the two ladies were actually pretty good, not that she was any real judge.

But Ben Hunter was awful. Purely awful! For some reason, that delighted her.

"I understand we're going to have a student exhibit at the end of the week," she said softly, leaning closer to Ben so that Perry the Paragon wouldn't overhear. He was wandering from table to table, scattering his pearls of wisdom. "Word of advice," she murmured. "If you enter this morning's effort in any exhibit, sign somebody else's name to it. That way nobody can hold you responsible."

He glowered at her, but midglower, his eyes warmed into a smile. "Yeah, it's pretty ugly, isn't it?"

"I wouldn't say it's exactly ugly…but then, I was taught that if you couldn't say something nice, it's better not to say anything at all."

He turned to reexamine his morning's work

while Maggie stepped back to study the man himself. If ever a man looked out of his element it was Ben Hunter with his bristly jaw, his honey-colored eyes and a pair of shoulders that threatened to burst the seams of his shirt. Not that artists couldn't be manly, but if Hunter had the slightest bit of artistic talent he was working hard not to let it show.

He raked his fingers through his hair, causing it to flop back on his brow. "Warm up exercise," he said gruffly. "I haven't painted in a while, so if you don't mind, I'll take a few days to get back in practice."

Yeah, sure you will. She thought it, but knew better than to say it out loud. No point in issuing a direct challenge. For all she knew, he might be really good, only not in any style she recognized. It looked like someone had dumped a bowl of scrambled green eggs on his paper and then tromped through it with muddy boots.

But then, her effort didn't look much better.

One of the women said something about the music, which was pretty cloying. "A little Vince Gill would suit me better," Maggie said.

"That reminds me, I understand there's dancing after dinner," said the woman with the pink hair. "There's a stack of old records, some of them 78s. Does anyone else remember those?"

Dancing, with a dozen women and three men to go around? That ought to be interesting, Maggie mused. They talked about music for a few minutes, and then a thoughtful Maggie wandered back to her own table. Not for the first time, it occurred to her that something about Ben Hunter didn't quite ring true. An artist, he wasn't. So why was he here?

The man would bear watching, she thought, and for some idiotic reason, found herself smiling.

Four

By mutual consent everyone migrated to the side porch, where a tray of glasses and another pitcher of tea was waiting, compliments of Ann, who seemed to spend more time in peripheral duties than she did in class. Could there be another nonartist who, for reasons of her own, had enrolled in Silver's circus? No wonder Silver spent so much of his time with the older members of his class. Apparently those were the only ones who were serious about learning.

Maggie felt Ben's presence even before he reached past her to scoop two glasses into the ice bucket. He filled them with the sweetened tea and handed her one, saying, "Here you go."

"Thank you," she said stiffly. Then, with false conviction, "This is really nice, isn't it?"

His eyes sparkled with hidden laughter. The journalist in her—not to mention the woman—wanted to ask him why he was pretending to be an artist when obviously he was no better at it than she was, and evidently no more interested in learning.

But then, he might ask a few questions she'd just as soon not answer.

He leaned against the porch rail, his gaze moving over the clusters of chattering women. She wanted to shout, *"I'm right here—look at me!"*

Instead, she backed away to perch on the arm of an Adirondack chair. The chair tipped, tea splashed over her lap, ice cubes skittered across the porch floor and Maggie swore silently. If there happened to be a spill, a splash or a drip anywhere in the vicinity, her body would attract it like a magnet.

When Ben leaned forward and began mopping at the icy liquid with a handkerchief, she shoved his hand away. "Don't bother. It's only tea, it won't kill me." Judging from what she'd seen of the facilities, any laundry equipment would probably consist of a washtub and a clothesline.

The older woman with the pretty pink hair strolled over. "Hi, you're Maggie and I'm Janie—I think we met yesterday. Are you having as much fun this morning as I am?" She held up her glass. "I don't think it'll stain. It's mostly sugar syrup." She kicked a few ice cubes under the railing without making a big production of it.

When Perry Silver joined them, the temperature seemed to drop several degrees. It had nothing to do with a few ice cubes melting in the shrubbery, or even the clammy mess plastered to her thighs. As uncomfortable as she was, Maggie sensed Ben's hostility.

Which was odd, as she'd never before been particularly sensitive to the feelings of others.

Well, except for Mary Rose. And her father. And the elderly widow she visited two or three times a week with library books and treats from the bakery. And maybe a few others.

"Are you enjoying yourself, Hunter?" Perry asked with a smile that easily qualified as a smirk.

"I was," Ben said. He hadn't moved a muscle. Maggie was reminded of a sleeping lion she'd seen at the Asheboro Zoo.

"Good, good." Turning to Janie, the artist said, "And you, little lady? This morning's effort showed definite promise. We'll have you painting like a pro by week's end, I guarantee."

Janie waited until he moved on to another group before murmuring a reply. "Sonny boy, if you're an example of a pro, I'll pass." With a shrug, she added, "He really is a good teacher, though."

"That's what everybody keeps saying," Maggie said. "Sure can't prove it by me."

When Janie wandered off to join Charlie and Georgia, Maggie turned to Ben, wishing she had half the poise of the older woman. Poise was tough enough when she was all dressed up in her Sunday best. Wet from the waist down, it was impossible. "Well...I guess I'll see you around."

Ben stood. He'd stood when Janie joined them until the older woman had pressed him back down again. Someone, Maggie thought—his mother, probably—had taught him good manners.

"Maggie," Ben said just as she was about to disappear inside. She glanced over her shoulder, and he grinned at her. "You're not all that bad. Honest."

"As if you'd know."

But she was smiling when she hurried to her room to wash off the stickiness and change clothes. Lord, the man was something. Trouble on the hoof. How was she supposed to concentrate on getting the goods on Perry Silver when all she had to do was catch sight of Ben Hunter for her knees to go weak and her brain to turn to gravy?

"Answer me that, Wonder Woman," she muttered.

Suzy was just coming from the room they shared, having shed the shirt she wore over her halter top as the day warmed up. Today's top was blue, and even skimpier than yesterday's. "What'd you say?"

"Nothing," Maggie snapped.

"I saw you drooling over our cowboy. Hey, there's going to be dancing tonight. Wanna draw straws for him?"

"This isn't drool, I spilled my tea."

"Whatever," the younger woman said with a knowing grin.

"Yeah, whatever," Maggie muttered as she hurried past to clean off the sticky mess. She'd do well to keep her mind on her mission.

A critique was no worse than the average root canal, Maggie told herself some forty-five minutes later, coolly admiring her own objectivity. Silver found something kind to say about almost every single work until he got to the last three examples, namely, hers, Suzy's and Ben Hunter's. After a lot of hemming and hawing, he called Ben's effort problematic, and to be fair, even Maggie could see that Ben's was easily the worst of the lot.

Silver would set up each student's work on his easel in turn. Then, using a brush handle as a pointer, he would indicate the parts that "worked" and those that didn't, and explain why. While Suzy's sky was nicely done and Maggie's colors weren't *too* muddy, evidently nothing in Ben's painting worked. Not a single thing.

Maggie put it down to jealousy. Both men were attractive, but there was really no comparison. Without lifting a finger, Ben attracted women of all ages. Maybe he was the son or grandson the older ones wished they'd been lucky enough to have, but there was nothing even faintly maternal in Maggie's feelings. Never having experienced it before, at least not to this degree, she recognized it as sheer, unadulterated lust.

"I don't know about you, but I kinda like my picture." Ben murmured in her ear, his warm breath sending tendrils of hair tickling her cheek—not to mention certain other ticklish parts of her body. "Reckon my granny would like to have it?"

"As a Halloween decoration, you mean? Tell me something—what is that wiggly streak across the front of the page? A rusty train track?"

"Now you're deliberately trying to hurt my feelings. It's a—"

Maggie never did find out what the jagged streak was supposed to be, as Ben glanced up just then and saw Silver in a huddle with the two women he had seemingly adopted. "'Scuse me," he said, and sauntered off.

Sauntered was a word Maggie rarely had an opportunity to use in her general advice column, but it came closest to describing that easy, loose-limbed way Ben Hunter had of moving, as if he were so comfortable in his skin he might actually fall asleep in transit.

Watching him make his way through the crowd, she could think of several methods she might employ in an effort to keep him awake.

Suzy sidled up beside her. "You think he's got a mother fixation, or whatever they call that thingee? Some kind of a complex?"

In Maggie's estimation, Suzy's four years at Chapel Hill had left her largely untouched, education-wise. But then, sometimes a college education took a while to filter through. As with whiskey, maturity often made a difference. She'd used that little gem of wisdom in one of her columns just last month.

"You mean Janie and Georgia? They're nice, aren't they?" *Be generous, Maggie—he could be going after Suzy or Ann.* "I wouldn't mind having either one of them for a mother."

When Suzy lifted one penciled eyebrow, Maggie shrugged. "My mother was never your standard cookie-baking, PTA-meeting, do-your-homework type of mother, if you know what I mean."

Suzy nodded, indicating she understood, then said, "Not exactly."

"Never mind. Look, how about doing me a favor? Remember what I told you about my friend, Mary Rose Dilys."

It was hardly a promising beginning, Maggie thought a few hours later as she dressed for supper—

starting with having to expose her total lack of talent, followed by a lapful of cold, sticky iced tea. After that came the afternoon session, which only confirmed what the morning class had hinted at. She'd bought the wrong kind of paint, the wrong kind of paper and her one and only brush was about as useful as a secondhand Q-Tip. Add to that the fact that of the only two men enrolled, the only attractive one—devastating, really—attractive didn't begin to describe him—preferred older women. As in about forty years older.

Catching sight of Ben and Janie wandering around outside while she tried to tame her hair, she thought, maybe if I were to use a rinse…

Her brush-hand fell still as she stared out the tiny window at the pair highlighted by the setting sun. Ben was definitely a saunterer, but Janie's walk defied description. Viewed from the back, with her pink, shoulder-length hair—which was really more of a peach-color—she didn't look a day over twenty-five. Maybe thirty. Even with those ugly cross-trainers. Heads together, the two of them were as chummy as a pack of Nibs.

Oh, well, Maggie rationalized, she hadn't come here looking for romance. From now on she'd pay strict attention to her mission, she vowed as she fished through her suitcase for something suitable for supper and dancing. Dancing was one of the few sports in which she excelled.

Lifting out her stiletto heels, she remembered the last time she'd worn them. She'd got one heel jammed between the boards in the deck of a nice couple who'd invited her to supper to meet their nephew.

No point in courting disaster. She'd be just as tall in her everyday platforms.

Suzy breezed into the room, still wearing her high-cut skintight shorts and the skimpy low-cut halter. "Hi, you getting ready for tonight?"

"For supper. I thought maybe—"

"Right. You thought maybe you'd get dressed up for the big diesel."

"The big—" Maggie felt her face grow warm.

Suzy said dryly, "You need to keep your eyeballs on a shorter leash. I mean, the man's a serious stud muffin, but he has this hang-up about older women. You said so yourself."

Maggie dropped back onto the cot. It threatened to tip and she grabbed the wooden sides. This was not her lucky day. "Are you going to do it?" she asked, referring to their earlier conversation.

"What, troll my bait in front of Silver?"

"Well, yeah…sort of. Nothing outrageous, but just let him know you might be interested. See how he reacts. In a house full of people you'll be safe enough, and I'll be standing by to rescue you if it comes to that."

"Now if we were talking about the mighty Hunter, I'd be way out ahead of you." She rolled her eyes. "Okay, okay. If things get too tense I can always take a cue from Ann and sneeze real loud." Their roommate had serious allergies.

Maggie sighed heavily. "It seemed like such a perfect plan when I started out. Now I've blown all this money—my dad's home alone eating junk food and smoking too much, and I'm not sure that even if I get proof that Perry's a—a philanderer, it will make a speck of difference.''

''A philanderer?''

''Skunk. The two words are interchangeable. My dad says I'm a meddler, but honestly, I'm not. It's just that I get these brilliant ideas that occasionally don't work out quite the way I'd planned.''

''Okay, I'll try my hand at being skunk bait. Beats working in an unair-conditioned office that smells like turpentine. I keep telling my dad that a window unit wouldn't exactly bankrupt James and James Lumber Company.''

''Who's the other James?''

Suzy grimaced. ''Moi. He hopes. You wearing that?'' She indicated Maggie's ankle-length, button-front, straight-line shirtwaist. ''Hate to tell you, but if you're looking for any action tonight, that dress has to go. Sexy, it's not, and besides, the skirt's too tight for line dancing. If those boots are anything to go by, that's probably all our cowboy knows how to do.''

Maggie tossed a Perry Silver Watercolor Workshop brochure at her. It sailed under the cot.

Seating arrangements had been slightly modified for the second night. Seated at the head table, Perry Silver had the only chair with arms, thus denoting his rank. Janie was on his right with Ben beside her, Georgia to his left, with Charlie beside her, with a retired public health nurse at the far end.

''How come all the men have to be at one table?'' Suzy asked as they made their way to the small table by the kitchen door. "Why can't we share the good-ies?"

"Ask whoever arranged the seating." Maggie wondered, too, but she wasn't about to make an issue of it. Charlie, she wouldn't have minded—at least he had a sense of humor, but either of the other two would have made her too nervous to eat, for entirely different reasons.

"I wonder how I'd look with pink hair," Suzy mused as she dug into the entrée, which tonight was pork chops and sweet potatoes with bagged coleslaw and biscuits from a tube, compliments of the two librarians and a retired accountant.

"If you mean like Janie's, it's more peach than pink."

"Whatever. Our cowboy sure seems to like it." She shot Maggie a sly look.

Our cowboy?

"So?" If she sounded preoccupied, it was because she was. Preoccupied with trying to keep her mind focused on the reason she was here.

Ann slid into the empty chair beside Maggie, her allergies apparently subdued. "I signed the three of us up for tomorrow, is that okay?"

Maggie said, "I thought when I signed up that meals were included."

Ann shook her head. "Read the fine print. Meals are provided, some assembly required. Words to that effect."

"If worse comes to worst I guess I could microwave," Suzy admitted.

Maggie sighed. "I can cook. Plain country, nothing

fancy. I've been doing it for years, else my Dad would have cholesterol up the wazoo."

Without cracking a smile, Ann said, "I didn't know there's where cholesterol settled. Live and learn."

"You probably didn't know Maggie was jumping off tall buildings to save the weak and helpless by the time she cut her permanent teeth, either," Suzy said dryly.

"Then I vote we elect her chief cook, you can do the serving and I'll do the bottle washing," Ann said. "Maggie? Okay with you?"

Maggie shot her a telling look. The fewer people who knew about her covert mission, the better.

They talked about men and about food and about the best shops in Hanes Mall. And about men again. "You know what?" Maggie said quietly. "I don't think he's all that great."

"Who, Ben Hunter? Trust me, he's great." The observation, not surprisingly, came from Suzy.

"I was talking about our leader," Maggie said. "Do you like his work?"

"Actually, he's considered quite good if you like realism—and lots of people do," said Ann, who seemed surprisingly knowledgeable considering she'd skipped most of the day's classes.

Maggie was about to mention a certain calendar in her father's office that reminded her of Perry's work when Suzy held up a hand. "Save it, we've got incoming."

He came up behind Maggie's chair. She didn't have to look around. Couldn't if she'd wanted to, not without brushing against him. Seated, her head was at belt level—or slightly lower.

"Hi," drawled Suzy. "You know everybody here, don't you, Ben? Ann, this is Ben—Ben, Ann. She came in late yesterday."

"We've met, thanks." Ben touched Maggie on the shoulder and she stopped breathing. "Got a minute? Something I'd like to talk over with you, if you'll excuse us."

Ann said, "Sure."

Suzy smirked.

Maggie was having trouble regulating her air intake, but she raked back her chair and followed him out onto the porch.

Fool, fool, fool!

Five

There was still enough of an afterglow from the spectacular sunset to cast shadows. "This really is a beautiful place," Maggie said brightly. She was nervous. Maggie was *never* nervous.

"Yeah, it's kind of pretty. Green, at least. Big change from where I came from." Ben sounded oddly distracted. He wasn't looking at the scenery, he was looking at Maggie.

"Which is?"

"Hmm? Oh—West Texas. Little town nobody ever heard of. It's pretty much flat if you don't count the anthills."

If anything could make her clumsier than she already was, it was feeling self-conscious, and the intent way he was staring at her made her wonder if the label at the back of her neck was sticking out. "I'm sure it's lovely," she murmured.

What she was sure of was that Ben hadn't brought her out here to talk about geography, his or hers. Why *had* he brought her outside? What could he possibly have to say to her that couldn't be said in front of the others?

"Maggie?" Was it her imagination, or did he sound as if he had a sore throat? He lifted his hands and dropped them.

She stopped breathing.

He lifted them again, and this time they made it all the way up to her face. Clasping her cheeks, he tilted her face up and lowered his own. Her eyes remained open until he went out of focus, and then all she was conscious of was the incredibly soft feel of his lips on hers.

Soft, warm, moist, they moved over her mouth, back and forth—undemanding. He didn't try to taste her, to involve her in anything more than a simple kiss.

Never—*ever*—had anything so simple been so complex.

He lifted his head and she wanted to pull him back, to lick his lips and then go from there—to follow this crazy thing that had blossomed inside her to wherever it might lead.

He cleared his throat. His hands rested loosely on her shoulders and his eyes, those warm whiskey-brown eyes, looked dark as night under his half-lowered lids. She couldn't have spoken if her life depended on it.

"How about you and me teaming up?" he rasped.

She blinked in confusion. It was the last thing she expected to hear. "You mean—cooking?"

He laughed, and it was as if someone had trailed a feather duster from the sole of her foot to the tip of her ear. "No, not cooking, although if you insist, we might give that a shot, too."

Omigod, he really was hitting on her. Teaming up. Was he talking switching roommates or…or something more permanent? "I'm not sure what kind of team you're talking about," she said cautiously, her head already reeling with possibilities. Would she or wouldn't she?

Well, of course she wouldn't. Where could they go for privacy? Besides, even without Mary Rose's example she knew better than to "team up" with a man she'd known for less than two days.

She stepped away, hoping she could think more clearly if he wasn't touching her. It helped…but not very much. Her lips still tingled and she wanted to feel it again—that incredibly soft pressure. She'd been kissed before, plenty of times—well, enough times so that she knew most kisses were pretty much alike. Open mouth, probing tongue, thrusting pelvis— the whole works.

Ben's kiss was totally different. The wild optimist hiding deep inside her pragmatic exterior wanted to believe he was reaching out to the woman she really was instead of simply reacting to a marginally attractive, marginally available member of the opposite sex.

He was no longer gazing into her eyes. Using the toe of his boot to dislodge a small rock from the red clay matrix, he said, "You might have noticed, I'm sort of out of my league here."

With his looks, he could hold his own in any league. He couldn't possibly be talking about…

"Oh…you mean art-wise?"

"Art dumb would be more like it." When he smiled, he had a crease in one cheek that almost qualified as a dimple. "You might even say I'm here under false pretenses."

The lawn immediately surrounding the house was unkempt—a little chickweed, a little grass and a lot of exposed rock. They reached the edge of the cleared area and Maggie waited for him to continue. Okay, this wasn't about sex. That kiss had been merely a—a bonding gesture. Like a handshake, only more personal.

It occurred to her belatedly that she might not be the only one here with an agenda that didn't include qualifying for membership in the Watercolor Society. Something was going on—something that probably didn't involve diving into the nearest bed.

Well…shoot!

She let him talk, trying not to notice the way he stood, with his feet braced apart in those well-worn boots and thumbs hooked into his hip pockets. Sort of an 'I-shall-not-be-moved' stance, with overtones of 'But-I-can-be-tempted'.

Yeah, right. Obviously she didn't have what it took to tempt him.

"See, I have this grandmother," he said.

Her jaw fell, and she snapped it shut. How did he get from a kiss that was like nothing she had ever experienced before to telling her about his relatives? Was he inviting her home to meet his family?

"Miss Emma—she likes for me to call her that—she's in her late seventies and lives alone. Not that she needs a caretaker or anything like that. I mean, she still does all her own housework, gardening—you name it. Gets involved in local politics, goes to these arts and crafts affairs. She just finished taking a computer class with some friends.''

Back to earth with a dull thud. ''So that's why you're here, right? You're checking this workshop out for your grandmother? Aren't there any workshops in Texas?''

''She lives in North Carolina.''

''Oh. Well, that's stretching family obligations, isn't it? Bringing a grandson all the way from Texas just to be sure a course is suitable? What was she afraid of, nude male models?''

He looked away, and she was tempted to grab that rock-bound jaw of his and force him to look at her. *I'm here—your granny isn't! Look at me, darn you!*

''See, she's taken all these classes in fancy sewing, lace-making, stuff like that. She goes to a lot of exhibits, too. Something to do with her time, I guess.'' He raked his fingers through his hair, dislodging a lock that fell across his brow. Maggie had already noticed that he did that when he was shaping his next statement. ''Anyway she told me about this guy she met at an art show last fall and how she came to buy a bunch of his pictures.''

''Paintings,'' Maggie corrected absently. ''When they're painted by hand they're called paintings.''

''Well, sure, I knew that.'' Ben rocked on his heels like a kid with a guilty conscience. Maggie thought it was endearing in a big, tough-looking guy from West Texas...or wherever.

''Thing is, these weren't real paintings, they were some kind of prints, I guess, but he wrote his name on them and sold a bunch of 'em. Miss Emma shot her wad buying one of everything. Things weren't even framed, just matted and sealed in plastic. Most of 'em looked pretty much like that thing Silver did this morning. Not much color, mostly browns and grays. Dead trees, log cabins, cornfields and patches of snow, maybe a mountain or two in the background.''

Now that she'd finally got her feet planted firmly on earth again, Maggie wondered where he was going with this. She didn't find Perry's work particularly exciting, either the one he'd done as a demonstration or those she'd seen hanging on the downstairs walls. But then, she was no art critic. Not yet, at any rate.

And neither, if his own effort was any example, was Ben Hunter.

''So you see where I'm going with this,'' he said.

''Uh…not really.''

Just then something small and dark swooped silently out of nowhere. Maggie flinched and hid her face. Ben grabbed her arm. ''Steady there,'' he cautioned. ''Some of those rocks are slippery—easy to lose your footing.''

Breathless, she said, ''It's not my feet I'm worried about. Was that a—a bat?''

''Not a bloodsucker, just the ordinary bug-eating kind. You didn't twist your ankle, did you?''

She was shaking her foot. ''I'm fine, stop fussing.'' She staggered slightly. She was wearing her clogs again. She'd packed only two pairs of shoes, not counting the old pair she kept in the trunk of her car for emergencies that were practical, but ugly as sin.

"I've got a pebble in my shoe," she admitted when the thing refused to fall out.

Ben squatted and took her foot in his hand. She grabbed his shoulder for support while he ran his finger between the platform and the sole of her foot.

"That's got it. I'm fine now, honestly," she said breathlessly. She'd be fine if he would remove his hands from her ankle and stop tickling her foot. On the other hand, if he wanted to kiss it and make it all better, she wouldn't complain.

When another bat swept past, she hardly even noticed.

Ben said, "You're sure?" He levered himself up, all six-feet whatever of lean, clean-smelling male. He really wasn't the handsomest man she'd ever seen, but there was something about him...

Maggie decided on the spot that starting tomorrow she would dig around in her car under the accumulation of junk and retrieve the hideous shoes with the thick soles, the padded tongues and the stripes on the sides. She'd tossed them in along with her space blanket, a flashlight and a first aid kit in case she ever got stranded on the road and had to walk. With her skinny legs, they made her look like Minnie Mouse, but then, even Minnie would have better sense than to go all mooney-eyed over a long-legged Texan.

"Could we get on with whatever it was you brought me out here to discuss? Something about teaming up?"

"Right," he said slowly, as if he were mentally skimming down a long page, trying to find his place. He was probably as rattled by that bat as she'd been, only being a man, he'd never admit it.

"You were telling me about your grandmother and her taste in art," she prompted when he stood there staring down at her as if he'd forgotten who she was, much less what he'd been about to tell her.

"Oh yeah. Well, like I said, Miss Emma's big on independence and all that. Once she retired, she bought herself an annuity and a bunch of CDs—not the music kind, the ones you get from a bank."

Maggie only nodded. There was probably a point here somewhere. Being a slow-talking, slow-walking Texan, it took him a while to get to it.

"Right. But then along comes this slick hustler, tells her one-percent interest or whatever she was getting, was peanuts. What she needed to invest in was art. In other words, his stuff. So bless her sweet, gullible heart, she cashes in a few CDs, throws in a couple of Social Security checks and buys herself a bunch of bad wallpaper, thinking she can resell it in a year or so at a huge profit."

"Why am I not surprised?" Maggie murmured. Any man who would sweet-talk a woman he'd just met with one eye on her trust fund would definitely do something like that. The old-fashioned term "gold digger" was usually applied to women, but it was definitely an equal opportunity appellation. Given enough material, she could write an exposé that might earn her a place on a real newspaper instead of a few double-column inches between Belk's white sale and the weekly specials at Mount Tabor Food Market. "How much did your grandmother, uh—invest?"

Why don't we try that kiss again? As long as I'm going to be remembering it for the next hundred years, I want to be sure I've got it right. Oh, and this

*time, put your arms around me. As long as I'm re-
membering, I might as well get the sizzle in all the
right places.*

"Get taken for, you mean? Not a fortune, but per-
centage-wise it was still way too much. Things cost
a couple of hundred bucks apiece, depending on the
numbers scribbled in pencil on the lower left-hand
margin. His autograph—"

"Signature," Maggie supplied. "You mean he actually puts the price right on the painting, or whatever?" She was finding it hard to concentrate on art,
much less on her personal mission—much less on *his*
personal mission—when he was standing there, looking so sexy and appealing. She didn't need the distraction, she really, really didn't.

"It's not exactly a price, but the numbers in the
left-hand corner have something to do with how valuable the thing is. Lower the numbers, the higher the
price, according to my source."

His *source?* This was sounding more and more serious.

"The one she paid the most for was marked eleven-
slash-one-twenty. Means there were only a hundred
and twenty of the things printed, issued, whatever you
call it—and hers was number eleven. Don't ask me
why it matters."

He took her arm and steered her toward an old-
fashioned wooden swing under a vine-covered arbor.
The fragrance of blooming wisteria was almost too
sweet. Maggie started to sit, thought about bees, and
stepped back, bumping into Ben. Excusing herself,
she sighed. "Look, could we just go inside where

there aren't any rocks, bees or vampire bats? I really can't concentrate when my life's in danger."

When it came to distraction, bats, bees and pebbles couldn't hold a candle to the man who towered over her. It wasn't enough that he was a supermagnet for any woman with a viable hormone in her body and that he could kiss like an angel—he had a granny he cared enough for to go the extra mile. That was like triple chocolate mousse—with nuts and brandy-flavored whipped cream.

"Sure, if you'd rather. I just didn't want to take a chance on being overheard."

"This is beginning to feel like a spy thriller," she said as she matched her short stride to his longer one. If he could ignore that kiss, than she could ignore it, too. It never happened. "You're not undercover for James Bond, are you?"

At the sound of his deep, rusty chuckle, she sighed. Okay, so it had happened. The guy was worse than an epidemic of Spanish flu. She was definitely going to need a booster shot, and the sooner, the better.

"Art police, you might say. Matter of fact, until about six weeks ago I was wearing a badge."

That stopped her cold. By then they'd reached the porch steps, with Maggie leading the way as if she could outrun temptation. Mounting to the top step, she turned. Ben was two full steps behind her, which meant for once she could look him square in the mouth—that is, in the eyes. And from the light shining out the window, his eyes were...

Oh, hell, Maggie, eyes aren't magnificent! Bodies, maybe—even faces, but eyes were just...

He was probably nearsighted. Or farsighted. What-

ever, no man was all that perfect. She said, "So
you're a cop." It sounded more like an accusation.

"Was. I resigned."

"You're too young to retire."

He looked away then, saving her from making a
fool of herself—again. "Let's just say it was time to
move on."

Well, that certainly rang false, but she knew better
than to try to pin him down, figuratively *or* literally.
Her hands might itch to touch that crease on his
cheek—or even the small scar on his jaw—but it was
an itch she wasn't about to scratch. "You know what?
Usually when someone begins a sentence with 'Let's
just say,' it means they're not telling the truth—at
least not all of it."

He turned to look at her again. "You know what?
Whenever someone starts a sentence with 'you know
what,' I figure they're getting ready to dodge the issue."

He moved up another step, which made her feel for
the step behind her. *Uh-uh. No way. You're not going
to draw me in with another kiss.*

Turning, she headed toward the far end of the
wraparound porch, where another wisteria-draped
trellis enclosed an old-fashioned wooden swing. The
place was booby-trapped!

Warily, she said, "You might as well tell me the
rest of it."

"Why I resigned?"

"That, too, if you want to, but I mean about teaming up. And your grandmother, and her being taken
in by…whatever."

"Bottom line—Silver might be a good painter, but

his real art is flimflam. I had a feeling something like that might be going on, but now that I've seen the way the enrollment shapes up, I'm dead certain. Didn't you notice anything unusual about it?''

"It's my first workshop, so I don't have anything to compare it to. If you're talking about the fact that six days of cooking your own meals and sleeping on a torture device costs almost as much as an ocean cruise, then yeah, I definitely noticed that.''

"Torture device, hmm?'' There was a long pause, during which her mind took off on a wild tangent. Then he said, "What I'm talking about—Silver's culled the applicants so he has just the right mix. Mostly women, mostly retirees.''

She waited for the punch line.

"What's the most vulnerable portion of society these days?''

"Babies? Kids who do dumb stuff and think it's smart?'' Women who get themselves kissed and are ready to send for the preacher? "I give up, who?''

"Senior citizens, that's who. Like my grandmother and all those other grandmothers he cons into signing up for his so-called art lessons. A captive audience, that's who. Give him a week to soften them up and he'll have at least two-thirds of them lining up to buy his pictures. He shook his head. "And yeah, I know—if they're done by hand they're paintings, but the ones he sold my grandmother weren't. The only thing done by hand was his signature in pencil, so if it's his autograph he's selling, why not just say so?''

"Because he's not famous enough, so nobody would want it?''

"Bingo. Trust me, I know what I'm talking about

here. I didn't just walk into this thing cold, I checked it out with a reputable source.''

She nodded knowingly. ''Reporters have sources, too. I could do some more checking if it would help.'' Not even to herself would she admit to being disappointed. He'd led her out into the moonlight to talk to her about teaming up. Could she help it if her imagination had slipped its leash for a moment? ''All right, so exactly what is you want me to do?''

''Just keep your ears open, that's all for now, and if Silver comes on to you, give him the brush-off. I want him to go after the older women, they're his real target. Before any damage gets done, I'll have him cold.''

Avoiding the shadowy swing, Maggie sank down into one of the cane rockers. It was already damp with dew. ''That's it? You can actually arrest him for trying to talk people into buying his art?'' She shook her head slowly. ''I don't know, Ben...''

Ben didn't know either. It wasn't like him to jump on his horse and ride wildly off in all directions without so much as a roadmap. It's just that when he'd realized that his own grandmother had been taken in by a scam artist, he'd seen red. Not until he'd signed up for this wingding and written a hefty check did it dawn on him that he couldn't just haul the guy in for making a sales pitch, even if he caught him in a flat-out lie. Fraud could be tricky as hell to prove. Not only was he out of his element with this art business, he was out of his territory.

Didn't even have a territory, for that matter.

''It's a work in progress, okay?'' he said. ''I'll think of something.'' He blew out a frustrated sigh, then inhaled deeply, aware of the heavy scent of the purple blossoms and the lighter fragrance of the woman beside him. "So, will you help me out here?"

He couldn't have felt more helpless if he'd been fifty miles out in the flats with a lame horse and no cell phone. Not that he hadn't worked with a partner before—he had. But this time his so-called partner wasn't a cop, and he didn't actually need her help. What he'd wanted to do when he'd led her out in the moonlight was kiss the living daylights out of her and go from there. Fortunately, after one brief sample, he'd had sense enough to back off. There was something about Maggie Riley that didn't add up. Whatever it was, it shorted out his brain and sparked a major reaction below the belt at a time when he needed all his powers of concentration.

Whatever else she was, Riley was a major distraction.

Touching his toe to the porch rail, he set the rocker in motion. A month ago he'd been holed up in an unused lineshack on a friend's ranch, firing off letters to the Attorney General's office, half expecting a sawed-off shotgun to poke through the door at any moment. Shoot, shovel and shut-up. It wouldn't be the first time a lawman had disappeared when he'd stumbled into something he wasn't supposed to see.

Maggie's voice came out of the shadows, yanking him back to the present. "The thing is," she said, "I sort of have my own mission."

"You're covering it for your paper? You said you were a journalist, right?" He was sitting far enough away so that there was no danger of touching her. It didn't help a whole lot.

''Well, that, too. I mean, I'd planned to write about it, but that's not why I'm here.''

''If you're wanting to learn how to paint, Janie says Silver's a better teacher than he is a painter. She says he's even a pretty good painter if you happen to like his style. From what I've seen, he paints the same scene, just rearranging the parts and changing the sky a little.''

''She's your special friend, right?''

Was that a wishful question? Ben stopped rocking, wondering how he could find out. They'd only just met. With some women, all you had to do was buy 'em a beer and it was off to bed, but Maggie was different. In spite of that impulsive kiss he'd stolen, she really wasn't his type. He usually went for long legs, big boobs and lots of bleached hair. Dolly Parton on stilts. Women who were good for a few laughs, a few rolls in the hay, but nothing more serious, because he was nowhere near ready to settle down.

Trouble with Maggie, the more he got to know her, the more he wanted to know. Whatever the attraction, it sure as hell wasn't her legs or her boobs. Although her hair was nice, even if it wasn't piled up like a bleached blond helmet. He had a sneaking suspicion she had brains and heart and all those other organs he tried so hard to steer clear of in his relationships with women.

''Yoo-hoo, y'all want some dessert?''

Saved by the bell, Ben thought. Good thing, too, because he didn't particularly like the way his thoughts were wandering all over the road. He was definitely losing his edge.

He said, ''Sure, Janie, what're you offering?''

Six

Dessert was store-bought cake that was too dry and too sweet. Maggie ate it anyway, because it was something to do and she was feeling edgy. Ben poured himself a glass of cold coffee, iced it, and stayed with her while the other stragglers left the kitchen and wandered into the large front room where someone was playing records. Not CDs, or even audiotapes, but vinyl.

Tapping rhythm on his glass with the blade of a table knife, Ben hummed along while Maggie finished her cake. He had a deep, gravelly voice—nice, actually, and only a few notes off-key.

"Care to join 'em?" he asked.

"Might as well," she allowed, feeling a shimmer of tension at the thought of dancing in Ben's arms. Slow dancing, not line dancing. Then maybe they would wander out onto the porch and he would kiss her again.

Several of the women were dancing together while Charlie looked over a selection of records, including some old 33 1/3s and even a few 78 rpms. Janie was dancing alone, clicking her fingers and swaying to the tune of something Maggie remembered her mother singing a long time ago.

Perry was nowhere in sight, nor was Ann.

Suzy came up behind them and said, "You wouldn't believe this record collection. If they weren't all scratched up, they'd probably be worth a bunch." She touched Ben on the arm and said, "Dance with me, cowboy. You don't mind, do you, Maggie?"

Maggie minded more than she cared to admit, but she smiled, nodded and knelt beside Charlie, who said, "Look at this, will you? I haven't heard this one since I was in grad school."

Maggie must have said something appropriate, but disappointment ate at her. Ed Ames tried to remember and the Mamas and the Papas went through their repertoire while Ben danced with Janie, with Georgia and with half the other women in the room, apparently having a wonderful time. She refused to look over her shoulder, but she could hear their laughter over the sound of the scratchy old records.

Someone called out, "Play 'Moon River' again, will you? It was my husband's favorite."

All dressed up and nowhere to go, Maggie thought, dismally amused. The dress she'd worn tonight was one of her favorites, bought on sale last fall. She hadn't been sure it would still be in style this year, but it was.

For all the good it did her.

Janie hadn't even changed for supper, much less for dancing. She was still wearing tights and a sweat-shirt, but she'd slipped off her shoes. She had bunions, Maggie noticed, and then felt horribly guilty for being jealous of a woman who was more than twice her age.

Charlie was still making discoveries in the stack of old vinyl when someone tapped her on the shoulder. "My turn," Ben said. "Charlie, stop hogging my woman."

Which was so totally absurd Maggie felt like taking a poke at him. Instead, she melted into his arms and they circled the small area that had been cleared for dancing. She couldn't think of a thing to say—nothing that made any sense, at least. She wasn't about to ask why he had danced with practically every woman there—with Suzy twice—before he'd remembered to ask her.

He was a surprisingly smooth dancer. Nothing fancy, just holding, swaying and shuffling, mostly, but she still liked the way he moved. The disparity in their heights should have made it awkward. Instead, she was in a perfect position to rest her cheek on his chest and hear his heartbeat.

Pa-bum. Pa-bum. Pa-bum, pa-bum, bum, bum, bum!

Evidently exercise got him all...exercised, she thought, savoring the thought that holding her in his arms might have something to do with his accelerated heartbeat.

His warm breath stirred her hair and when her left arm got tired of reaching up to his shoulder, she looped it around his waist. The record—one of those old LPs that had half a dozen different songs on each side—shifted into something with a jazzy beat, but Ben's rhythm never changed. Slow and slower, feet barely moving at all, they swayed in place.

Maggie was aware of little outside the feel of his lean, hard body, the scent of one of those fresh-smelling soaps, and the thump of his heart under her cheek. She was pretty sure the shape of his hand would be branded on her back for weeks. She could have drifted this way forever, not thinking beyond the moment.

Ben started to hum again. The sound—more a vibration, really—triggered a response in parts of her body that had no business responding to sound. Under her dress she wore only a pair of briefs and a silk camisole. Her breasts, as small as they were, seemed to swell as if begging for attention. Her nipples actually throbbed.

When the record finally came to an end, Ben led her toward the French doors that opened out onto the porch. His breathing was audible, even over the murmur of conversation coming from three of the women in the corner who had set up a table under a yellow bug-light and were playing gin rummy.

Suzy had evidently given up and gone to bed. Maggie wondered if she should feel guilty for hogging the most attractive man on the premises for so long.

No way. Regardless of what happened next, the last hour was going to be tucked away in her memory box for a long, long time. Her life wasn't exactly a hotbed of romantic moments.

By silent mutual consent they headed for the swing this time. Ben's arm was still around her as if he'd forgotten where he'd left it. She hadn't forgotten, not when every cell in her body was dancing the cha-cha-cha. Nearby, a whippoorwill tuned up. Through some trick of acoustics, she could hear the sound of sporadic traffic out on highway 52, several miles away as the crow flew.

Pausing in the shelter of the wisteria vines, Ben turned her in his arms. "Maggie, there's something you need to know."

I already know everything I need to know, she thought. I know I'm in serious trouble if you're not feeling the same way I am. I know I've never been so attracted to any man before, not this soon. I know I've got no call to accuse Mary Rose of—

"Hey, do you two *mind?*"

The sound of Charlie's voice was like a dash of ice water. Ben tensed, but didn't release her. Maggie, her face burning, tipped her head forward to rest on his chest.

Ben said, "Sorry, man. I didn't know the swing was taken."

Maggie said, "It's late anyway." She pulled away, fighting disappointment. "I'd better—that is…"

At first she thought he wasn't going to release her, but in the end he let her go with a quick kiss on the top of her head. "Tomorrow," he promised. Actually, he only said it, but she wanted desperately to believe it was a promise.

She didn't slam the door. She didn't even stomp as

she made her way though the house to the glorified
pantry where she was billeted. She had long since
outgrown childish tantrums, but that didn't mean
she'd outgrown being disappointed, much less being
sexually frustrated. She *wanted* the man. She hadn't
actually wanted a man since...

Since never.

Suzy was adding another coat of polish to her toenails. Glancing up, she raked back her short hair and
grinned. "I thought by now you two would be getting
down to some serious kanoodling."

Maggie slipped off her sandals and reached for the
shirt she wore to sleep in. "Try finding any privacy
in a house with fifteen people."

"There's always the basement or the attic."

"Forget it, I didn't come here to waste time kanoodling."

So much for all her splendid plans to spare Mary
Rose from heartbreak and poverty.

"Wanna talk about it?"

Maggie hung up her dress, and without turning
around, said, "I don't even want to think about it."

She slept like a log and woke hearing the sounds
of laughter coming from the kitchen. Evidently, Suzy
and Ann were already up, dressed and ready to start
cooking breakfast for anyone who wanted something
more than dry cereal. Feeling guilty, Maggie dashed
upstairs, waited for a shower to be free, and then hur-
riedly dressed, this time in her oldest jeans and a yellow camp shirt that was wrinkled from being
crammed in her suitcase under a box of graham crack-
ers. She tucked her damp hair behind her ears and put

on a tinted lip balm. If anyone thought she was going to take any special pains with her looks on account of last night, they were sadly mistaken. Anyone being Ben Hunter.

As early as it was, several people had gathered in the front hall to watch a uniformed man laboring up the front path carrying a large carton. Charlie said, "If that thing's as heavy as it looks, we're going to have a seriously herniated brownie here."

Ann had already brewed the coffee and Suzy was staring at the big iron skillet as if she'd never seen one before.

"Hey, can somebody take this thing and sign for it?" the deliveryman called through the front screen door.

Ben came in from the side porch and said, "Sure thing. Let me help you set it down." If he noticed Maggie's presence, he ignored it.

She shrugged off a stab of disappointment, although she didn't know what else she could have expected. Nothing had really happened between them last night. Occasionally she got swept away by her own creative imagination.

As Silver had yet to put in an appearance, Ben signed for the delivery and tipped the deliverer, which Maggie considered generous of him. Charlie said, "Don't try to pick it up. Those guys know how to carry stuff like that. You can throw your back out without half trying."

"What is it?" Janie murmured from halfway down the stairs. She looked fabulous. Maggie made up her mind on the spot that if she had to grow old, she was going to use Janie Burger as a pattern.

Charlie obviously liked her style, too, she thought, remembering the two of them swinging away on what she'd come to think of as her and Ben's private place.

Janie leaned over and studied the label on the carton. "Hong Kong? Jeepers, who does he know in Hong Kong?"

But by then the first batch of bacon was starting to burn. Suzy yelled for help and Maggie hurried back to rescue it and to start whipping up eggs. The delivery was forgotten as talk turned to today's assignment and other esoteric topics, such as whether or not Ginko biloba improved the memory, and the lack of anything but white bread.

Perry arrived late. He seemed distinctly put out on finding the front door partially blocked by the delivery. "Leave it," he snapped when Ben offered to set it out of the way. "Where's Ann?"

"She made the coffee, but she was sniffing and sneezing. She's probably gone back to the room," said Suzy. "Have you had breakfast yet?"

Instead of replying, he stalked off in the direction of the room the three youngest class members shared. Maggie nearly scorched the eggs, wondering what was going on. It wasn't the first time she'd noticed the interaction between Ann and the instructor. She'd even asked about it, but Ann had brushed off the question and asked, instead, what being a reporter was like. Not that she'd seemed particularly interested in the reply, but then, when Maggie got onto a topic that interested her, she tended to lapse into essay mode.

Janie and Georgia offered to help clear up after breakfast so that they could all get started on today's assignment, which was painting on location. "I'm sorry, dears, but they're predicting rain starting late tonight, so I've decided to push things along a bit," Perry had said by way of explanation.

"I could've told him it was going to rain. My bones gave me fits last night, I couldn't sleep a wink," remarked one of the retired teachers.

Maggie had had trouble sleeping, too, but more on account of painful thoughts about Ben than painful joints.

Painting on location turned out to involve dragging all their gear from the studio outside. A few students produced clever contraptions that appeared to be a combination stool and easel, but most, including Maggie, were assigned card tables which were neither large enough nor steady enough to be practical. The second time her water pail sloshed over, Ben suggested she either dig holes for two of the legs or prop up the other pair.

"Smart, aren't you?" She flashed him a nasty look that had him grinning. "I already thought of that."

It would probably have occurred to her sooner or later, but she enjoyed sparring with him. At least it helped dispel the awkwardness after last night.

Ben helped Georgia find a place that was more or less level, helped her set up her equipment, and then helped Charlie wrestle a heavier picnic table into the shade for the two librarians. For all he looked like the hero of one of those action movies—rough, ready and more than slightly dangerous—Ben Hunter was a genuinely kindhearted man. He would make some woman a wonderful—

Don't even go there.

"Ann's going to work inside today," Suzy said

when Maggie asked about their roommate. "Pollen count's too high."

One of the blue-haired ladies mentioned that the coming rain would probably help reduce the pollen count, never mind how it affected various joints and sinuses. Soon they were all busy rendering the mountain scenery in a medium that had Ben cursing and Maggie muttering about paint with a mind of its own.

"Look at that!" she snarled after some twenty minutes had passed. "The blasted paint refuses to stay where I put it! The sky keeps washing away my mountain and when I try to push it back up where it belongs, the darned stuff fights back!"

"Here comes Perry, he'll tell you what you're doing wrong." That from Georgia, whose sky was behaving the way a sky should instead of trickling down the mountain where there wasn't even a valley, much less a blasted waterfall.

"This is for the birds," Ben growled. He stepped back, hands on his hips, and glared at the buckling sheet of thin watercolor paper.

"That reminds me, we'd better watch out for dive bombers." Charlie nodded toward a flock of grackles squabbling over a stand of pokeberry bushes.

"Purple, right? Couldn't hurt. Might even help." Ben happened to catch Maggie's eye. He winked and gave her a thumbs-up, his thumb stained with what she now recognized as alizarin crimson.

Where the dickens did he see anything red out there? Was he color blind?

Wearing a crisply ironed smock and his usual beret, Silver meandered among his students offering a word of advice here, a compliment there. He went lighter than usual on criticism, which in Maggie's estimation was a good thing. It wouldn't take much for her to throw everything into her hatchback and head home, mission or no mission. Suzy had reluctantly agreed to cooperate, but so far Silver had shown surprisingly little interest. Today he ignored her completely, probably figuring that like Maggie and Ben, she was beyond help.

Instead, he spared most of the time and attention for his older students. Not Charlie—not Janie or Georgia, either, but as they were all adequate painters, they didn't really need him. Janie, in particular, had a style Maggie liked. She called it her ''who gives a hoot, I'm having fun!'' style.

Silver spent most of his time with a small group of students who lapped up his every word as if it were nectar. Ben caught her eye and nodded at the cluster of appreciative women. At least his mission appeared to be on track.

A few minutes later Silver moved to the edge of the rough lawn, stepped up on a low granite outcropping and clapped his hands for attention. ''All right, children, lunchtime is critique time. When you're finished here, make sure your work's dry and take it in to the studio.'' He glanced at the sky. ''Leave everything else outside, we'll try to squeeze in another hour after lunch before the rain starts.''

There were a few groans, but the overall response was muted excitement. Evidently artists were masochists, willing to endure everything from gnats to glaring sunshine to swollen ankles and aching feet for their art.

Ben tucked something in his shirt pocket, rolled up

his morning's work, dry or not, and joined Maggie, who was scowling at the mess she'd made on a perfectly good piece of white paper.

She said, "Is there some secret to keeping your skies from wandering downhill and messing up your mountains?"

"What you have to do, see, is learn to go with the flow." He draped a companionable arm across her shoulder. The magic was still there, but today there was an added quality. A sort of best-buddies warmth that was almost—not quite—as potent.

"I read that on a T-shirt somewhere." It had been her mother's T-shirt, worn with a long, flowered skirt. Come to think of it, long flowered skirts were back in style again. Going with the flow never would be, not as far as Maggie was concerned. She had too much ambition. Too many people depending on her. If she went with the flow the way her mother had done, her dad would end up living on junk food and clogging his arteries and Mary Rose would probably end up broke and brokenhearted.

"What's that in your pocket?" she asked, watching the rocky terrain carefully so as not to trip. She didn't have a whole lot of dignity left; she'd just as soon hang onto whatever she could salvage.

"Show you later," he promised, which only perked up her curiosity.

Seven

It was devastating. Maggie laughed aloud at the caricature of a willowy man in a beret and a flowing smock. His long, thin nose was exaggerated, his eyes baggier and too close together, but the resemblance was striking. "I thought you said you didn't have any artistic talent."

"I don't. A friend of mine is a police artist and she taught me a few things. Mostly she used composites in her work, but she had a great eye when it came to summing up a particular set of features."

Maggie tried to see Ben through the eyes of a caricaturist—or a police artist. The way his thick, dark hair grew, with that bit he was always shoving back off his forehead. The winged curve of his eyebrows, the angular cheekbones, a nose that was not too big, but not too small, either—and the shape of his mouth.

Oh my, yes, the shape of his mouth…

She wanted to ask what else the woman had taught him—if he'd had a special relationship with her and if so, what had happened to it.

None of your business.

She had her own past, such as it was; he had his. If there was one thing she'd learned over the years since she'd first noticed that boys were a different and rather interesting species, it was that the really good-looking ones were usually vain and immature. Not that many of the really good-looking had given her a second glance, much less asked her out on a date.

Suzy was setting out sandwich components when they reached the kitchen, "Where's Ann?" Maggie asked. She got out a pitcher of iced tea and opened the freezer compartment. "She said she'd help."

"Dunno. Her coffee mug's missing, so maybe she's back in the room."

After filling a bucket with ice, Maggie slipped away to check on the missing member of the team, trying to remember anything she'd read about allergies that might be helpful. Ann wasn't in the room they shared, nor was she in the studio. Maggie dashed upstairs to check the bathroom, called a few times in both directions, then hurried back down to do whatever else was needed. Lunch was usually a do-it-yourself meal, but the team-of-the-day was supposed to make the process easier.

"Maybe she drove into town for a prescription or something." Suzy was layering cheese, onions and peanut butter on a poppyseed roll.

Maggie stared at it and shuddered. "If she's smart she'll have lunch while she's out. Who did the grocery shopping for this place? Why isn't there any low-fat mayo?''

"How about rye bread? Next time anybody goes to town, how about picking up a loaf?'' Charlie asked.

Bumping elbows, begging pardons and discussing everything from arch supports to the best source of ready-cut mats, everyone pitched in before wandering away, sandwiches and drinks of choice in hand.

Suzy and Maggie remained in the kitchen, finishing off leftover slices of cheese and a box of stale vanilla wafers.

"I might as well clean out this peanut butter jar. We can open a fresh one tomorrow,'' Suzy said.

Maggie picked up wafer crumbs with her thumb. "Wonder what Perry meant when he asked if we could touch our toes. Was he trying to be cruel? I mean, just look at this class—most of the women probably wear support hose, and the men aren't much better.''

"Charlie might wear support hose, but I betcha Ben doesn't.'' Suzy grinned, leaned back in her chair and stretched her arms. "Be glad to check it out for you, though. Wasn't that what you were wanting me to do? Check out the guys?''

"One guy only,'' Maggie reminded her.

"Oh, yeah, I keep forgetting.''

"Surrre you do,'' Maggie teased.

Once the kitchen was put in order, the two women joined the others in the studio where the morning's efforts had been laid out on the tables, ready for a critique. Maggie pointedly didn't look at Ben, but her peripheral vision was excellent. He stood, feet braced apart, hands on his narrow hips, silently challenging Perry to do his worst.

Perry was just hitting his stride when someone near the window noticed that it had started to sprinkle outside. In the rush to rescue whatever had been left behind after the morning's session, Maggie heard Ben tell the two women at his table to stay put, that he'd collect their things.

And that was another thing—he was so darned decent!

She beat him to the front door by half a step and was headed down the wet steps when he caught her by the waist and swung her to the ground. Over her protests he said calmly, "Crazy shoes, slick steps, sure recipe for disaster." He set her down on the broken concrete walk, then jogged off to gather up anything the rain might damage. Staring after him, Maggie had a sinking feeling that the kind of trouble she was in had nothing to do with slick steps and three-inch platforms.

"What about your boots?" she called after him.

Without turning around, he waved a dismissing hand and began gathering up painting equipment. Maggie glowered. "Talk about vanity, there's not a horse within fifty miles of this place."

Suzy dashed past her, both arms full, a knowing grin on her piquant face. "Oh, shut up," Maggie grumbled. Grabbing the supplies she'd left on her rickety card table, she glanced around to see if anyone needed help. The rain was falling harder now, plastering her hair to her head, her shirt to her back. Dodging others on the same mission, she collected whatever she saw that looked in need of rescuing and hurried back inside.

Charlie helped her unload and distribute materials, then Ben came up behind her, laid a big, warm hand on her shoulder and said, "You get everything in? Need me to go back out and bring in the rest?"

"Thanks, I'm fine," she said, sounding breathless and hoping he put it down to exertion. "I guess we don't need to worry about the tables."

Charlie grumbled, "Maybe I should've left my morning's work out in the rain. Couldn't hurt—might even help. Did I tell you about the time I was painting on a dock down in Southport and a gull flew over and made a deposit on the seascape I was working on? Actually, it didn't look too bad. I had to wash off some of the texture, but the gray cloud worked out pretty well."

Ben chuckled and placed his hand on Maggie's back, ushering her into the front hall where the others were examining their belongings for rain damage. A rash of goose bumps shivered down her spine, radiating outward from his hand. She ducked away and was considering dashing back to her room for a dry shirt when a loud thump sounded from overhead. Several people looked up. One woman fingered her hearing aid.

Someone said, "Thunder?"

Charlie said, "Perry dropped his attitude?"

"Sounded more like he dropped a load of bricks," offered a woman whose work Maggie had admired in yesterday's critique.

Before anyone could go investigate, Perry appeared

at the head of the stairs, attitude intact. "No problem, dears, just some paper I had delivered."

So that was what was in that carton. Maggie had heard all about the advantages of three-hundred-pound watercolor paper over the cheap pad she'd bought at the discount store. She hadn't thought it meant the stuff literally weighed three hundred pounds.

Rubbing his hands together, Silver beamed down at them. "Everyone finished with lunch? Good, good—shall we get on with the afternoon session then?"

"Do we have any choice?" Ben muttered softly.

"Amen," Maggie echoed. Considering how much it was costing her, she really should try to get something out of it. So far, she hadn't collected a speck of evidence that would convince Mary Rose that this skunk was risky marriage material. All she'd learned was that she had the wrong kind of paints, the wrong kind of brush and the paper she'd paid nearly ten bucks a tablet for was barely a step up from newsprint. Evidently imported was the only way to go.

Add to that the fact that she was highly susceptible to slow-talking, slow-walking Texans who were also totally out of their element, and she was in so far over her head she needed a snorkel just to breathe.

Ann slid into place almost an hour into the afternoon lesson. Maggie didn't hear her approach, as the rain that had started shortly after noon drummed steadily on the roof so that it was hard to hear anything at all.

"Hi. We missed you this morning," she murmured, noting that the young brunette looked even more tired than usual. "I set up your stuff there on the end of the table. We've been working on graded washes. You've studied with Perry before, haven't you?"

Without answering, Ann said, "I think I'll pass. My hands are—that is, my head's really stopped up."

At the other end of the eight-foot table, Suzy swiped a wet brush across the streak of burnt sienna and tipped her paper up the way Charlie had shown her. After his opening demonstration, Perry had spent most of his time with a retired dental technician and the two librarians.

"Hey, you know what?" Suzy whispered. "I figured it up last night. Not counting room and board, each one of these so-called classes is costing us eighteen dollars an hour. Multiply that by fifteen. What I want to know is, how much is overhead and how much is pure profit?"

"Are you sure you don't want to manage your father's office?" Maggie teased. "I can probably name one of the operational expenses—liability insurance. My dad does that sort of thing."

"How's your wash coming along?" Ben joined them after glancing over at the instructor, who was still holding his elderly students in thrall. "Hi, Ann, you feeling better?"

Ann's gaze slid away. She mumbled an excuse and left the room. Ben shrugged and looked after her. "Was it something I said? Suzy-Q, this little place right here's not working." He waved a big, square-palmed hand over what was supposed to be a graded wash, but looked more like a fallow field after a deluge.

Suzy struck a pose, batted her lashes and thrust out one shapely hip. "Do me a favor, Texas—stuff it in your saddlebags."

Ben grinned, flashing that not-quite-a-dimple again. "Yes, ma'am."

Something that felt uncomfortably like jealousy churned in Maggie's stomach. But then, with Suzy's figure, she could have read the label on a can of motor oil and made it sound like the *Kama Sutra.*

Maggie didn't have a figure. She'd reached the pinnacle of figurehood at the age of thirteen and been stranded there ever since. With enough makeup she could improve on her face, but she drew the line at enhancing her bustline, surgically or otherwise. Occasionally she used a temporary rinse, but it was hardly worth the effort as the result was simply ordinary Maggie with different colored hair. Unadorned, at least she blended into the scenery, which was a definite advantage for an investigative reporter. Beauty faded. Brains only grew sharper. She'd been telling herself that for years.

Janie wandered over and tucked her arm through Ben's. She'd ponytailed her hair, making her look like a teenager whose face had inadvertently been left too long in the water, causing it to pucker.

"I'm thinking of adopting him, ladies. What do you think? I can't talk him into eloping with me, but I'm not about to give him up."

Ben kissed her on the cheek and winked at Maggie. "I'll have to introduce her to Miss Emma. Might make for a pretty interesting relationship, right?"

He was a magnet, no two ways about it. Suzy latched on to his other arm while Ben, the big jerk, just stood there soaking up adoration like Roy Rogers after he'd saved Dale Evans from a fate worse than death.

If he said, "Aw, shucks, ma'am," Maggie vowed silently, she might do him serious bodily harm.

"Children, children, time's wasting. Now, let's see how we're doing with our graded washes, shall we? Suzy, doll, I'm afraid you weren't listening. You must—now listen, class, this is crucial—you simply *must* learn how to master your medium, otherwise it will get the best of you every time. Watercolor's not like oil or acrylic—it won't just sit there meekly and let you push it around. You must be *trick-y, trick-y, trick-y* if you want to master watercolor!" Perry was fond of speaking in triplicates.

Trick-y, trick-y, trick-y, Maggie mimicked silently, feeling distinctly uncharitable at the moment. Let's just see how masterful he was when Mary Rose and her humongous trust fund slipped through his fingers.

While Maggie, Suzy and Ann, who showed up again after class, began putting together the evening meal, Ben sat at the kitchen table and entertained them by drawing quick caricatures. Janie was easy— Charlie, too, as he was the only other man in the class besides Perry. The rest weren't quite as easy to iden tify, but everyone got a laugh as they picked out the one they thought represented them.

Maggie looked at the figure that was supposed to represent her. Was he trying to be kind? Afraid of hurting her feelings? She was the original stick-figure, but instead of drawing her that way, he had given her a sexy shape and a headful of wavy hair.

She didn't have waves, she had a shaggy cut and dozens of cowlicks. And surely her eyes weren't *that* large.

When she glanced up, all ready to ridicule his efforts, he was tipped back in his chair, hands laced across his flat belly, staring at her. From any other man, toward any other woman, she might even call the look smoldering. A practiced pragmatist, Maggie put it down to either distraction or a possible astigmatism.

Charlie spoke up admiringly. "Hey, man, you're good."

"Who's good?" Perry joined them without his usual Perry-like entrance. Quickly searching the room, he pointed toward Maggie, Suzy and Ben. "You, Maggie—and you, darling—you, too, Hunter. A few of you still haven't caught on. Tonight after supper, we'll talk about some of the physics involved."

The *physics?*

Maggie glanced at Ben, this time for reassurance and not whatever it was that set her hormones to sizzling whenever he was around.

Ben shrugged and mimed, "Beats me."

Then Perry leaned over and murmured something quietly to Ann, who slipped away, leaving the salad for Suzy to finish.

Knife in hand, Suzy turned to Ben. "Help out here, cowboy. Grab me an onion from that sack." She did a perfect Mae West, complete with a modified bump and grind, the only difference being a few years, a few pounds and the paring knife in her hand.

Maggie managed to produce a passable vegetarian

chili, one she'd often served her father. Dessert was canned peaches, and as no one complained—at least not in her hearing—she felt free to relax. Ann never reappeared, not for the meal itself or for the clean-up after. Maggie was seriously starting to worry. If her allergies were that bad, she didn't need to be here.

Between finishing the dishes and assembling for the evening session, Maggie settled into the porch swing and gave it a gentle shove with her toe. The rain had stopped, leaving behind a layered fog that reminded her of the cover of a Gothic romance. All it lacked was a veil-clad heroine fleeing some unspecified evil.

Stealing a moment to brace herself before facing Perry's criticism, she shoved off with one foot. She wasn't really surprised when Ben appeared, caught the chain and held it still long enough to settle in beside her.

"You think Ann might be allergic to this house?" she asked.

"Could be. It's old, probably full of all kinds of mold spores. Now she's complaining about her hands, too."

"Pretty young to be a hypochondriac."

Maggie set the swing in motion again, needing an outlet for the restless energy that always seemed to assail her whenever he was near. All along the shadowy porch others were settling in the rockers and Adirondacks. One or two perched on the railing.

Ben inhaled deeply. "Something smells good."

She opened her mouth to tell him it was the wisteria, but she heard herself saying, "Insect repellent."

Anything to break the spell that was stealing away her objectivity. "Where's Suzy?" she asked brightly.

"Haven't seen her in the past few minutes."

Feeling his gaze on her, she tried to act like the adult she was instead of the adolescent she had never quite left behind. "Maybe she's with Perry. I guess it's time to go back in."

"Jealous?"

She planted both feet on the floor, causing the swing to jerk on its chains. "Of what?"

"Hey, just because the guy's a crook, that doesn't mean women don't like him. Part of the problem is that they like him too much."

"Yes, well this woman thinks he's a creep." And then, because she felt guilty for not leveling with him after he'd told her about his grandmother, she blurted, "If you must know, my best friend thinks he's in love with her."

Long pause. "And?"

"Well...I don't think he is, that's all."

"Because...?"

How could she explain tactfully? "For one thing, she only met him once for a few hours, and I'm pretty sure she hasn't seen him since then."

"You don't believe in love at first sight?"

Maggie set the swing in motion again. As Ben wasn't ready, the movement was jerky. Well, shoot. With a moon creeping over the mountain, layering the valley with silver veils of fog, any woman with half a brain would know how to take advantage of the moment.

Not Maggie. Oh, no, not Maggie the klutz, Maggie the skinny kid whose hottest date in her senior year had been with a certified nerd who'd taken her to a science fair.

"Look, my friend just happens to be rich, all right? I mean her father's this big pickle magnate and she's as sweet as she can be, and I don't want to hear any jokes about sweet pickles. With the name Dilys, she's heard every pickle joke in the book. The thing is, she doesn't know a lot about men."

Some of her belligerence faded when Ben's fingers closed gently on the back of her neck, pressing ever so slightly. It hurt, but in a delicious way. He said, "And you know all there is to know about men, hmm?" Finger-walking along her tense muscles, he said, "Don't you ever relax?"

For a few heavenly moments she let him work at untying the knots at the base of her skull because it felt so good, and because his voice was murmuring abstract words that didn't seem to relate to anything. Before she could melt into a disgusting puddle of liquid desire, she cleared her throat and said, "Uh— where was I? Oh yes, Mary Rose. Well as I was saying, her father's so overprotective he still vets all her dates. She's twenty-five, for goodness sake! You'd think we were back in the Dark Ages." Closing her eyes, she let her head roll forward as Ben worked his magic. "Ah, right there…"

Against the creak of the swing and the murmur of voices farther along the porch, a whippoorwill tuned up for his evening serenade. Maggie shifted slightly so that Ben's hand left her neck, his arm resting along the back of the swing.

"I'm probably overreacting, but you see, she's always let her folks run her life. I keep telling her, you don't learn anything that way."

"Who runs your life, hmm?"

She had to smile. "Me. At least since I graduated from kindergarten. Okay, maybe from the sixth grade." His fingers brushed her hair again. She would have moved away, but moving required too much energy. To cover what could only be called a stealth attack of lust, she said, "Mary Rose graduated from college with honors. Besides that, everybody always says she has the prettiest face, and she does." If she sounded slightly belligerent it was only because she was trying to stay focused in spite of a major distraction.

"So where's the problem?" His fingers brushed her nape, then moved through her hair. Did hair have nerve endings?

Hers obviously did. That's what came from having the dead ends whacked off every six weeks. "The problem is—" she said, ignoring the urge to curl up in his arms and let nature take its course "—the problem is that I think Perry's only after her money. Maybe I'm doing him an injustice, but if she marries him and finds out he's not what she thought, it's going to break her heart." As an advice columnist, she had heard the same sad tale too many times. About the way men changed after marriage. All the promises they made before and how quickly they were forgotten once the honeymoon ended. Broken promises that led to broken marriages and broken hearts, never mind the poor children left broken and bewildered in the wreckage.

Think about all that, Maggie Riley, and stop think-

ing about jumping into bed with a man you've known for all of two days!

"Let me see if I've got this straight," Ben murmured, his fingers slowly massaging the back of her head. "You're going to rescue this woman whether or not she wants to be rescued, right?"

Instinctively, Maggie pressed her head against his touch. "Isn't that what you're doing for your grandmother?"

"Nowhere close. I was too late to keep Miss Emma from getting snookered. Best I can do is spare other grannies from the same fate by reminding this jerk that there's a thin line between hyping a product and fraud, and he might have stepped over it when he started touting his pictures as investments."

"Fine. You do your thing, I'll do mine. And I'm really sorry about your grandmother, but that's already done. If I can keep Mary Rose from being married for her money—and don't tell me he's truly in love, because from what I've seen, Perry Silver wouldn't know love if it jumped up and bit him on the keester."

Ben's hand fell away as he started to laugh. Maggie could have sunk through the floor. Here she was sharing a swing with the handsomest man east of the Mississippi, with a big moon coming up over the mountain and wisteria blossoms perfuming the air, and what did she do?

She blew it, that's what. No wonder she'd never had a serious relationship in her entire life, if you didn't count the one that had ended in the back seat of Larry Beecham's Pontiac when she was seventeen.

Go with the flow, her mother used to say, espe-

cially after she'd enjoyed one of her hand-rolled cig-
arettes.

Maggie had never learned to go with the flow.
She'd been too busy fighting the waves. Hiding from
her parents' noisy arguments. Keeping her father's
spirits up after his wife left him—reading all those
articles about depression and leaving them where he
would be sure to see them. Studying hard so that in
case she could scrape together enough money to go
to college she'd be eligible. Taking courses in the
local community college and working for a miserable
little freebie paper for a pittance while she waited for
a chance to get on with a real newspaper.

"Maggie?" Ben's raspy drawl crawled down her
spine sending shock waves to the most vulnerable
parts of her body.

"What!" she snapped. And then, letting her head
fall back again, she closed her eyes. "I think I'm
having a premature midlife crisis."

"You'd be surprised what we could do if we
teamed up." The words were whispered. Just as the
meaning sunk in, his face went out of focus, and then
he was kissing her again. And not just any old kiss,
but one of those magical Ben-kisses—incredibly soft,
warm and moist—pressing, lifting, moving so that she
wanted to climb onto his lap and have her way with
him.

And he wanted the same thing, she could tell by
the way his heart was thundering. Or was it hers?

She was in way over her head, drowning in a sea
of desire. Without lifting his face from hers, he drew
her onto his lap. She tugged at his shirttail, hungry to
touch his body—to slide her hands over that broad,

warm chest. To press herself against him, to follow wherever he led—

To lead the way…

From inside came the sound of music from the old wind-up Victrola as someone opened a door. Maggie opened her eyes wide. Breaking away, she gasped, "'Scuse me," and reluctantly pulled free.

He didn't try to hold her. She thought she heard him utter a swearword, but he might have been laughing, instead. She had no intention of hanging around long enough to find out. She wasn't rated for this much temptation.

In fact, she'd do better to head for the studio so that Silver could tell her what a miserable failure she was as an artist. At least her ego wouldn't suffer, because it wasn't involved.

He chuckled, which was just as bad. The mere sound of his voice saying anything at all punched all her buttons, including a few she didn't even know she had. "Like I said before, why don't we team up?"

She turned to confront him and discovered that he was closer than he'd been only moments before. "How? You want to catch him selling a bill of goods to Janie and Georgia and the others. I want to catch him trying to seduce Suzy and get it on tape."

"Which is illegal," he reminded her gently.

"Whatever. I just don't see how we can do both, do you?"

Eight

Half an hour later, Ben glanced into the living room where Charlie was entertaining the ladies by playing disc jockey. Maggie wasn't there. Probably just as well. He had some thinking to do, and clear thinking wasn't an option as long as Maggie was anywhere around.

What the devil was it about the woman, anyway? Technically speaking, she wasn't particularly pretty. Over the years he'd arrived at certain standards, and Maggie Riley didn't meet a single one. So why was it that he could look at her from across the room and be so turned on he had to pull his shirttail out and hope it covered the evidence.

Not only that, but he liked hearing her laugh. Liked hearing her talk—got a kick out of her irreverent comments about Silver and his pretentions.

Hell, he just liked being around her. Trouble was, just being around her wasn't enough, and that was a distraction he didn't need.

The sound of laughter came from the large room they used as a studio. From somewhere else in the house he heard the strains of something jazzy and pictured Maggie kicking off her shoes, snapping her fingers and moving to the music.

Why not join her? Maybe do a little moving himself?

No way. Given a choice of hearing Silver blow him off as a no-talent jerk or making even more of a fool of himself with a woman he barely knew, he opted to use the rare privacy to sift through what little evidence he'd collected. So far, most of it was circumstantial, including the discreet sign announcing that signed and numbered prints would be available for sale at the end-of-the-workshop exhibit. Not signed and numbered copies, which might have given him something to go on.

Okay, so maybe he was crazy. Maybe he was totally off-base. But when Miss Emma had told him how much she'd spent, and he'd checked around and found out that her chances of ever recovering her investment were about as good as his chance of being elected president, he'd had to do something.

It boiled down to shades of gray. The ones here were paler than the ones he'd uncovered in Dry Creek, but people were still getting hurt. People like Miss Emma who had done nothing to deserve it.

Both in his law career and on the streets before Mercy had hauled his butt out of the fire, Ben had seen about every shade of gray there was. He didn't like any of them, but only a fool believed the world was all black and white. That didn't mean he could quit fighting gray where he found it.

And then there was Maggie, whose face kept getting in the way of his deliberations. With Maggie Riley, what you saw was what you got, which might even be a part of the attraction. Because what he saw was a small, gutsy woman with an understated brand of beauty all her own. Whatever it was, it could sneak up on a man and zap him with a sucker punch before he knew what hit him.

Ben had a long-standing policy, based on the experience of his friends, of keeping his personal life impersonal. What he hadn't counted on was a small distraction by the name of Maggie Riley.

Lying there half-asleep, he pictured her as a skinny kid in wrinkled tights, a mask and a homemade cape, determined to save the world. She must have been a real handful growing up. Still was, come to that. Super Woman minus the tights and cape, determined to save a friend from being hoodwinked by a smooth-talking flimflam artist. Oddly enough that was also his goal. Trouble was, they might need to take different routes to get there.

Charlie came in while he was still picturing Maggie in different costumes, mostly filmy, lacy stuff that enhanced rather than concealed.

"Hi, sport, d'you get your message? You left your cell phone on the dresser. It was ringing when I came in before supper."

Ben sat up and raked his hair back. "You're looking bright-eyed and bushy-tailed."

The older man grinned. "Here's hopin'," he said

cheerfully as he changed into a clean shirt, splashed on a palmful of Old Spice and checked his billfold. "You seen that moon yet? It's a doozy."

A doozy? Right.

Ben levered himself out of bed and retrieved his cell phone. He'd quit wearing the thing since he'd come east. Didn't know of anyone who might try to reach him unless it was Miss Emma, calling to remind him to eat a good breakfast, wear a raincoat if it clouded over and put on a sweater if it turned cool.

While he was checking to see if he recognized the number, Charlie said something about not waiting up. Ben nodded absently. He recognized the area code. And then he recognized the number.

Charlie said, "Wish me luck, sport. It's been a while."

"Yeah, sure," Ben muttered. Now why in hell would Internal Affairs be calling him? He'd turned over everything he had, knowing it probably wasn't going any farther up the ladder. He might as well have buried it in a time capsule.

With one last glance in the mirror, Charlie said, "Nothing serious, I hope. I tried to find you, but you weren't in the house."

Ben glanced at his watch. Even with the time difference it was too late to call back. He'd like to think it was only a glitch in the paperwork. He'd misspelled a name or failed to cross all his *t*'s. He glanced up and said, "Yeah, sure—thanks, Charlie. Uh—you going out somewhere?"

The older man sighed and shook his head. "Ben, Ben, Ben—wake up and smell the flowers, boy. Life don't last forever." He closed the door quietly behind him, leaving Ben in a cloud of aftershave to ponder a few more imponderables. Like why I.A. would suddenly want to contact him. They'd grilled him thoroughly, going over and over every speck of evidence before he'd been allowed to leave Dry Creek. By that time, sick at heart and mad as hell, he'd felt like a traitor for turning in fellow cops he knew and liked and had once respected. He'd grilled steaks with several of the guys, even attended the christening of their kids.

But that was before he'd happened to see a couple of the older ones deliberately turn away at a critical moment so as not to witness a crime going down. Wondering what the hell had happened, he'd started to tackle them on it, but something had stopped him. That crazy sixth sense that warned an experienced cop when something was out of alignment.

Over the next few months he had quietly observed certain transactions taking place in dark alleys, in empty buildings—even on the damn country club golf course. That's when he'd realized just how high up the ladder the rot went. Feeling like a traitor but knowing he had no choice, he'd gone first to I.A., then to the chief himself. He owed him that much and more.

"Figgered you had us made, boy. Always was a smart one, that's why I hauled you out of that gang before you got in too deep."

At fifteen, Ben had been running with a gang of jackers, doing body work—mostly disassembling and filing off VIN numbers. Another few months and he would have been in too deep. Alvin Mercer, called

Mercy by those on the right side of the law, had taken his age into consideration and gone to bat for him.

What made it worse when Ben had confronted his mentor with indisputable evidence was that the chief hadn't even tried to deny it. If anything, he'd seemed almost relieved. "Times a man goes along to get along, son, but it don't pay. Nosiree, in the long run, it's more trouble than it's worth."

So now here he was, an unemployed ex-cop, more than a thousand miles from home, taking a damned art workshop in an effort to catch some creep who was ripping off senior citizens by mislabeling a product.

Old habits died hard. Some never died at all. One of the last assignments he'd worked before pulling the roof down on his own head was the classic borrowed-bank-account scam. Working with a veteran officer—one who'd been clean, incidentally—they had set up the scene. Three days later the mark had taken the bait. This good-looking kid had approached Abbie, who was dressed in civvies and sitting in her car in the bank parking lot pretending to be adding up a deposit before going inside.

The perp had walked up and introduced himself and asked if she could help him out, explaining that he was new in town and his mama had just sent him a check to live on while he interviewed for jobs. Trouble was, he didn't yet have an account and the bank wouldn't cash his check.

Eight out of ten times the women fell for it. The perp would hand over the check, the woman would deposit it in her own account, withdraw the amount—usually a few thousand—and hand it over. A day or so later she'd hear from the bank that the check she'd deposited was no good. Not only was the account phony, the bank it was written on didn't exist.

Ben had warned his grandmother against the borrowed-bank-account scam, but he'd been too late to warn her against investing her life's savings in a bunch of pictures that were supposedly guaranteed to triple in value in a year's time.

He'd smelled a rat as soon as she'd told him what she'd done. Just to be sure—hell, he knew as much about art as he did about toe dancing—he'd gone online and checked out a few things. Then he'd placed a call to an art teacher he'd met when her fifteen-year-old kid got in trouble for shoplifting.

Mona Hammond had summed it up for him. There were legitimate prints, several different types whose names he couldn't recall—some of them extremely valuable, depending on the artist and the rarity. But if an artist painted a picture and then had copies made, then the copies were just that. Copies. Names and numbers scribbled on the margin didn't change the fact that they were no more valuable than the knockoff Rolexes peddled on street corners.

"That's not to say that some of them aren't lovely," Mona had told him. "But even when they're printed on all rag paper using the finest quality inks, they're still technically reproductions, copies of the original painting."

"What about as an investment?" he'd asked, and she'd just laughed.

"No way, hon. I might buy one if I liked it and wanted to live with it, but then, that's the best rationale for buying any art. I wouldn't recommend buying one as an investment, though. So, when are you coming back home? We miss you here. Mike was asking about you just the other day.''

He'd told her his plans were still on hold and hung up, wondering just when his life had taken a turn for the bizarre.

Unlike Maggie, Ben hadn't grown up with a save-the-world complex. Instead, he'd grown up on the streets of a small town that had started out as a farm community more than a hundred years ago and grown when a big manufacturer had moved in. He barely remembered his father, although he clearly remembered driving all the way to North Carolina with him in a pickup truck with a busted muffler to meet Miss Emma. Just him and his old man. He must have been about eight or nine.

It had been like dropping in on another world. They'd stayed about a week before heading west again. His father had been a long-haul truck driver, gone more than he was at home. One day he was gone for good. Just forgot to come home.

Ben's mother hadn't been much on discipline, either her own or her son's. When she'd been arrested on a drug charge a year or so later, a social worker had called Miss Emma, who had paid his fare east. He'd stayed with her until his mother was released. A few years later when she'd skipped town with one of her boyfriends, Ben had stayed on in their trailer until it had been repossessed, then moved into an empty warehouse, which was how he came to get mixed up with the jackers.

If he hadn't been bailed out by Alvin Mercer, a heavyset, soft-voiced cop who went on to become chief of police, he might have ended up doing hard time—or worse. Instead, he'd ended up going back to school and eventually wearing a badge.

Years later he'd been compelled to rat out his mentor and most of his friends on the force. God, he'd hated that! He happened to know Mercy had been trying to hang on until retirement, fighting prostate problems and a few other symptoms that had him pushing more pills than a backstreet dealer. Ben would like to think he'd done the chief a favor, but some days he still felt lower than pond scum.

He wondered what Maggie would say if she knew about him. About where he'd come from and what he'd done back in Dry Creek. He wondered if she'd consider him a traitor or just a guy trying to do the right thing in a situation that was neither all black nor all white, but too many shades of gray.

He finally drifted off, half-thinking, half-dreaming of a crime-fighting duo wearing midnight blue capes, uncovering scams and writing them up in comic book format.

Sometime in the night he roused enough to roll over, aware of the faint sweet, spicy scent and the sound of someone humming softly. At that point his dreams took a decidedly different track. Just after daybreak he woke drenched in sweat, his pulse pounding like a jackhammer. Charlie was snoring in the bed across the room. Without arousing him, Ben collected a handful of clean clothes and tiptoed down the hall to shower and shave before going in search of caffeine.

The first class wasn't scheduled until nine, but the new cooking team was already in the kitchen when he followed the tantalizing aroma of dark-roasted coffee. The pot was institutional size. A few hardened addicts would be drinking the stuff all day, but after the third reheating, Ben couldn't handle it.

"Yes, ma'am, three strips if you don't mind, and however you're cooking the eggs this morning, that'll be fine, too."

The cook-of-the-day patted him on the shoulder. "Sit down, honey, I'll have it for you in a minute."

Breakfast and lunch were served in the kitchen; dinner in the dining room that also served as a gallery for Silver's art and a few select pieces of student work. Ben was still musing on what it would have been like to grow up in a home with a mother who cooked breakfast and called him "honey" when Maggie wandered in, looking as if she hadn't slept any better than he had.

Considering the part she'd played in his early morning dreams, Ben thought it was no wonder she was looking kind of used up. Wearing her clunky toe-ring sandals with a shapeless blue dress that covered her down to the ankles, she still managed to look sexy as hell. Wet hair had left damp patches on the shoulders, as she hadn't bothered to dry it, much less use those fat rollers and sticky sprays his last lady friend had used. Maggie's hair, roughly the color of desert camouflage, usually looked like she'd stepped outside in the wind and forgotten to brush it when she came back inside.

On Maggie, it looked good. Everything about her looked good.

In his usual place at the end of one of the long kitchen tables, Ben remembered his manners and lurched to his feet. There was room to spare, but she bumped against his shoulder on the way past. "You're blocking traffic," she muttered, her voice gruff with sleep. "Where's my mug?"

"Morning to you, too, sweetheart." He sat down again, wondering what she'd do if he hauled her down onto his lap and stroked her until she purred. He might be tempted to try it if it weren't for a room full of chaperones.

"Has Ann been in yet?" Maggie asked the woman who was lifting bacon from a fourteen-inch iron skillet.

"Lord, yes, she was in here when I came down to start the coffee. She'd already made herself some instant—I think she might've taken it upstairs."

Aware of him with every cell in her body, Maggie ignored Ben as she poured herself a mug of coffee, diluted it with milk and added two spoonfuls of sugar. One mystery was solved, anyway. Last night when she'd gone to the room they shared, Ann had been nowhere in evidence. According to Suzy, she was up on the third floor doing office work for Perry to pay for the workshop. "Ask me, she's not getting much for her efforts. I doubt if she's spent more than five hours in class since we started." Suzy had gone on patting moisturizer on her throat.

"I don't know...that thing she painted yesterday looked pretty good to me. Better than Perry's, anyway."

Shrugging, Suzy had said, "So maybe we should change teachers. By the way, when are you going to stop hogging our cowboy? Perry won't give me the time of day, so I might as well have some fun while I'm here if you're not interested.''

Oh, Maggie was interested, all right. Which was not to say she intended to do anything about it.

That had been last night. Now, sipping her coffee, she tried to remember whether or not she'd answered. At the time she'd still been under the spell of that romantic, wisteria-scented fog, wondering what would have happened if the two of them had been alone instead of surrounded by fully half the class.

Disgusted, she dumped in another spoonful of sugar and reminded herself that, while imagination was a great advantage for a novelist, too much of the stuff could pose a danger for an objective journalist.

She stole a glance at Ben, caught him looking at her and lowered her flushed face.

Cool, Maggie—really cool.

Just then Perry made his entrance, pausing in the doorway to beam at his audience. ''Morning, morning, morning! Remember the first day when I asked how many of you could touch your toes?'' Without even looking around, he accepted the steaming pottery mug of coffee someone handed him.

General groans were heard. Several more people had wandered in during the past few minutes. ''What is this, the inquisition?'' asked a woman in a flowered muumuu.

''Methods, methods, methods,'' Perry sang. ''Loose, loose, loose!''

''Trick-y, trick-y, trick-y,'' Suzy said, snickering just loud enough so that several people turned to look at her as she reached for a cup. She'd applied lipstick and eye shadow, but hadn't bothered to brush her hair. On some women, Maggie thought rancorously, bed-head looked good.

Pointing at the far end of the long table, the instructor indicated a group of four women, all well past middle age, none with any noticeable degree of talent. "Remember yesterday when I told you that the object of art is not to copy nature, but to comment on it? To interpret what you see? A few of you seem to be having problems with the concept."

"Does he mean we're supposed to color outside the lines?" Maggie whispered.

"Maybe he should practice what he preaches," Suzy replied. "You see the way he interpreted that old barn hanging in the front hall? He even painted the splinters in the wood and the shadows under the rusty nails. Might as well use a camera with a close-up lens if that's the kind of interpretation he wants. Be a lot faster, that's for sure."

One of the cooking team set a plate on the table before him and Perry took his seat and applied himself to breakfast. "Thirty minutes," he warned, fork poised over the mound of scrambled eggs. "Everybody be ready to make great strides today."

Yesterday's efforts were still spread out on the tables when the class straggled into the studio. Rather than face a critical review, Maggie tucked her drab, colorless blobscape under her tablet. As an artist, she was hopeless. Even Suzy was better. The only one worse was Ben Hunter, who didn't give a hoot. Maggie probably shouldn't, either, but then she'd always hated to fail at anything.

"It's the quality of your paints, Maggie," Janie

said softly. "Too much filler. Let me give you a few tubes of artists grade paint, it'll make all the difference in the world."

"Thanks, but it won't, not really. I shouldn't even be here."

"I was wondering about that," the older woman said with a lift of one carefully penciled eyebrow. "There are some excellent beginner's classes available in Winston. Had you thought about signing up for one at the Sawtooth Center?"

Before she could come up with a reply that wasn't an outright lie, Perry waltzed into the studio brandishing his brush as if it were a baton. "All right, ladies…and gentlemen," he added as an afterthought. "Now, here's what we're going to do today, even those of you who don't need loosening up. It won't hurt and it just might help give you a different perspective."

"The hell it won't hurt if it's that toe-touching crap." Charlie's grumbling voice could be heard all the way across the room.

Perry glared at him. Then, lifting his drawing board from the table at the front of the room, the instructor dropped it onto the floor, a fresh sheet of three-hundred-pound d'Arches already taped in place. Beside it he set his water pail and his big messy palette. "Now, bending from the waist—" He swayed from the hip several times in case anyone was in doubt of the location of the waist. "I want you to *swe-e-eep* in the sky, using plenty of color in a big, juicy wash!"

He demonstrated with a few broad strokes, clearly visible to those at the front tables. Those in the back of the studio hadn't a clue.

"You, Mr. Hunter—are you amused at something I said?"

"Who, me? Amused? I was just wondering why anyone who wants to can't sit on a chair and straight-arm down to the floor. Get pretty much the same result, wouldn't we?"

"*Must* I explain all over again? We need *free*-dom of movement. That simply can't be had sitting down."

But when three women left the room and returned with kitchen chairs, he only shrugged and went on with his demonstration.

Some forty minutes later as the class broke, some moving to the front of the studio to view the morning's masterpiece, others heading for the doors, Ben came up beside Maggie and slipped an arm around her shoulders. "You gotta admit, what he did this morning looks a hell of a lot better than these things he's got hanging on the wall. If that's an example of loose, I like it a whole lot better than tight."

Maggie felt as if someone had touched her with a live wire. Somehow she was going to have to drum up some resistance before she did something foolish. "I wouldn't know, since I couldn't see past all his admirers," she said, trying for blasé and missing it by a mile. And then, "Ben…" She looked up and found herself captured by his warm brown eyes. "Um—Charlie looks like he's coming down with something. You think he might be catching whatever Ann has?" She hated it when her voice sounded as if she'd just run a three-minute mile, but that was the way Ben affected her. Maybe she was the one with the allergies.

"He was out late last night. Probably just needs more sleep. C'mon, I want to show you something."

"Out where? What about the next assignment?"

Ben just shrugged. "It'll wait."

"Where are we going?" Not that she cared as she hurried after him. Obviously, mountain air had a deleterious affect on the immune system.

He led her out the back door, away from the house, to the vine-covered arbor. "If you're talking about the view," she said breathlessly. "I saw it the other night, remember?"

What if he tried to kiss her again?

What if he *didn't?*

So much for her powers of resistance.

"You put fifteen people—sixteen counting Silver—in one house, and it's damned near impossible to find any privacy."

Her breath snagged in her lungs. He *was* going to kiss her again! Her lips softened in expectation.

And then he reached into his pocket and pulled out a sheet of paper that looked as if it had been crumpled, smoothed out and then folded. Without another word, he handed it to her.

Puzzled, Maggie stared at the scribbled words, all in pencil, all similar, but with slight variations. "What am I supposed to see?"

"What does it look like?"

Trying to hide her disappointment, she looked again, frowning. "Somebody practicing cursive writing?"

"Try again."

"A...signature?"

"Bingo," he said softly. "And who needs to practice a signature?"

"Physicians?" she said half-joking, still puzzled. She looked up to see him smiling down at the top of her head. The smile faded from his mouth, then from his eyes last of all, leaving in its place something edgier.

"How about forgers?" he said softly.

Nine

"You're kidding, right?" Still holding the scrap of paper, Maggie searched his face. "You're not kidding," she said softly. Thunder echoed in the distance. Neither of them noticed.

"On a scale of one to ten, this probably rates about a two. This art scam, I mean." A slight breeze ruffled his hair, tempting her to smooth it back from his brow.

"If it is a scam." Regardless of what he'd said, Maggie, as an objective journalist, tried to keep an open mind. Marrying a wealthy, inexperienced woman for her money was one thing, but art forgery? She didn't have a clue. "How can it be forgery? Those prints hanging on the walls are obviously Perry's work. We've both seem him painting pictures that look almost identical. They've all got his signature. In fact, come to think of it, on the prints—re-productions, whatever—he's written his name twice, once on the picture itself and once in the margin. So what's the problem?''

"I'm not quite sure, but I intend to find out," he said grimly. His face softened and he continued to look at her.

Her breath quickening, Maggie waved away a bee that seemed more interested in her hair than in the nearby blossoms. Another rumble of thunder rolled across the valley. Forcing herself not to stare at his mouth, Maggie said, ''So what do you think? He's practicing bending over from the waist to sign his name?''

"Hold still," Ben murmured.

She froze, her eyes darting to the nearby arbor, half expecting an armed forger to be lurking in the shadows.

Armed with—what, a loaded fountain pen? All this talk of forgers and scams was distracting her from her primary mission.

Slowly, Ben lifted his hand to her head. He said, "Shoo." And then he growled, "Scat, dammit."

A bee lifted off and droned away, moving heavily, as if it had pigged out on nectar. Ben went on staring at her hair. He said, "Raw sienna."

She blinked. "Raw what?"

"Your hair. I've identified three of the colors, but this one right here…I'm not quite sure." He fingered the tendril of hair she had tucked behind her ear as it dried. "There you've got your burnt sienna, your burnt umber and your yellow okra—it's this one right here I can't quite identify.''

"Ochre," she corrected absently. The class had not entirely been wasted on her. "It's called yellow ochre."

"Yeah, that's what I said. I figure you've got all the colors they used in the desert cammy uniforms."

"Am I supposed to thank you for the compliment, or whack you and march off in high whatchamacal-lit?"

"High gear?"

"High dudgeon. It's what ladies and English but-lers are known for in regency romances." And then, before he could come back at her, she closed her eyes. "Forget I said that, will you?"

He laughed, and just like that, all thoughts of forg-ers, gold diggers and desert camouflage evaporated.

But not romance, regency or otherwise. For one tingling moment Maggie's world narrowed to include only the man who was standing so close she could see the shards of gold in his whiskey-brown eyes, the iridescent gleam in his crow-black hair and the crease in his left cheek that was almost, but not quite, a dimple.

Without thinking, she reached up and touched it. He caught her hand and held it against his face. Heat sizzled between her skin and his. Just before he low-ered his lips to hers, she heard him whisper, "This is crazy…"

This time there was nothing tentative about the kiss. It was carnal right from the start. And it felt so good, so right in the cool, fragrant morning air. She only wished she were taller so that everything would fit better. It occurred to her that if they were lying down, everything would fit perfectly.

But misaligned height had nothing to do with taste, and he tasted like coffee and mint and something wildly intoxicating. When his hand moved up and down her back, cupping her hips, she wanted to rip off her clothes to allow him better access. Her meager breasts swelled eagerly as his hands moved over her body.

And then he discovered that she wasn't wearing a bra and the exploration expanded. His thumbs feathered across her hardened nipples, zinging messages to the place between her thighs, preparing her for what was about to happen…

Only it wasn't. It couldn't. Not in broad daylight, in plain view of anyone who happened to glance out the window. Maggie could have wept with frustration. Never had she been kissed so thoroughly, so deliciously. Never before had she realized what a potent instrument a tongue could be.

Slowly, Ben lifted his face to stare down at her, his breath as ragged as her own. "Come on," he whispered roughly, and before she could protest—not that she would have—he led her through the patch of mountain laurel down a narrow path.

"Where?" she panted, barely able to keep up.

"Waterfall," he said. He stopped, turned, and drew her into his arms again. This time when the kiss ended there wasn't the slightest question of where they were headed.

Someplace private. Someplace *very* private.

Someplace where they wouldn't shock anyone who stumbled across their naked bodies. Because sure as the sky was blue—well, gray at the moment, and getting grayer—they were going to be naked and all over each other the minute they found a patch of level ground.

It was level only by comparison. Covered with dark green moss, surrounded by rocks worn smooth by time, it was barely wider than her cot. Ben lowered her and followed her down. Somewhere nearby, Maggie could hear the sound of moving water, but she had eyes only for the man kneeling beside her. With a soft oath, he ripped his shirt off over his head. Cloud-filtered sunlight splintered off his powerful shoulders.

He said, "Maggie…?"

"Yes." Just that one whispered word. It was all he needed; all either of them needed.

Buttons and zippers were dealt with, and Maggie waited impatiently while Ben tugged off his boots in order to pull off his jeans. Wearing only a scrap of yellow lace—lingerie was her one secret indulgence—she lay back on the velvety moss and watched as he finished undressing.

His hands were shaking. For some odd reason, which she didn't even bother to explore, that made her feel empowered. Mighty Maggie strikes again. Weak men fall to their knees; brave men quail in terror.

There was nothing faintly weak about Ben Hunter. Even in areas where the sun couldn't reach, his skin was the color of a rich latte. Flat black curls T-ed across his chest and arrowed down toward his groin, where…

"Oh, my," she whispered as he tossed his jeans aside and came down over her.

"Don't talk—don't think." His voice sounded like torn canvas. "Just let me…"

She couldn't have spoken then if her life depended on it. So she let him…and he let her. Coals that had smoldered since the first time she'd noticed him when he'd been leaning into the cab of his truck quickly burst into flames. In a single moment, Maggie went from being a mature, sensible woman to being a wild, irresponsible creature, heedless of all but her own burgeoning needs. Oblivious to the warm breeze that played over her naked body—to the cool moss beneath her, she was conscious only of Ben's arms, his hands—his fiercely aroused body moving over hers.

Her hands fluttered over his back, urging him on. *Now, now—please!*

He took his time. His mouth drove her wild with a series of soft, maddeningly gentle kisses before tracing a path of wildfire down her heated body.

"Please?" she managed to squeak when his lips moved over an exquisitely sensitive place.

"I—wait a minute," he said gruffly, and pulled away.

Frantic with need, she clutched at him as he reached over to drag his jeans closer. "Don't you dare leave me now," she cried softly.

"I used to carry—not sure it's still there, but—"

And then he was back, and she closed her eyes.

Ben suited up swiftly, his hands unsteady, his heart thundering visibly. He knew something about explosives, but never had he experienced anything as incendiary as the touch of this one small woman. If they'd both been dressed in asbestos it wouldn't have mattered. One kiss—one touch, and he would have gone up in flames.

He moved over her again, parting her thighs to kneel between them. "Beautiful," he whispered raggedly. "So beautiful."

He kissed her eyes and her throat, inhaling the intoxicating scent of soap, shampoo and aroused woman. He kissed her breasts, paying homage to the small pink nipples that rose hungrily to meet his lips. He placed kisses in the hollow beside each hipbone and one on her soft belly before moving on. By the time he lifted himself over her again, her heels were softly pounding the earth. She was whimpering with need.

And he was trembling with it. "I want it to be good for you, sweetheart," he said huskily.

"Yes!" she exploded, pulling him down to her with small, but surprisingly strong hands. Those were the last words either of them uttered until the wildfire died away.

As soon as either of them was able to move, Ben rolled onto his back, taking her with him. She lay draped over him like a damp blanket. If she was anywhere near as replete as he was, neither of them would be moving for the next few days.

Thunder rumbled across the mountains. A cool draft stirred the treetops around them. Once his breathing returned to normal, Ben whispered, "Maggie...I think it's about to rain on us."

"Mmm."

"You want to head back?"

She shook her head—managed to do that much, at least. "Uh-uh."

Eyes closed, he grinned. "Me, either."

She felt a drop of rain on her bottom. Just one, though. And she felt him stir to life beneath her. This time, since she was already on top, she took the line of least resistance.

Neither of them spoke on the uphill trek to the house. Maggie probably because she was too winded, Ben because he knew better. Anything a man said at a time like this was apt to land him in trouble.

He thought it, though. *What the devil have you done to me, woman?*

If she had any idea he was thinking things no cop, ex- or otherwise, should be thinking about, she'd high-tail it down the mountain. The odds were lousy. Four of the seven men he'd worked with over the past ten years had at least one busted marriage behind them. A couple more were in counseling. Hell, even in a small town like Dry Creek, where most of the problems were either drug-related or domestic, the stats were lousy.

And he was due back there on Monday. Barely time enough to throw a wrench in Silver's smooth little operation and say goodbye to Miss Emma. No time at all to figure out what was going on with Maggie, much less to try and explain why it would never work.

Who was it who'd said something about east being east and west being west, and the trains never running? One more pothole in his formal education.

Maggie marched past him without a word. Probably had a head full of second thoughts herself. Pure devilment made him call after her. "Hey! See you in class this afternoon, right?"

No reaction.

Just as well.

Charlie was in the men's john trying to wash a spot of something off one of his shirts. "You missed lunch," he said. "I don't know who made the last supply run, but we're already running short of a few things. I put down rye bread. You showering now? Didn't you shower this morning?"

"Poison ivy."

"Bad stuff. They got a washing machine in the basement if you want to use it. Be sure you use hot water, though, else it just spreads the oils."

Ben stepped in the shower stall and turned on the water to keep from having to lie any more, either by omission or commission. He had a feeling that if he were to look the older man in the eye, Charlie would be able to see right through him.

Maggie had never been so confused in her life.

Actually, she had, only not about sex. She was hardly promiscuous, but neither was she wildly experienced. Of all the men she had ever slept with— all three of them—no one had ever made her feel the way Ben had. Just thinking about him made her feel warm and gushy all over.

Class was already in session by the time she showered and changed into her last clean outfit. She should have packed more clothes and fewer snacks, but then, live and learn.

She slipped into the studio just as Silver was winding up a demonstration. Suzy made room for her and whispered, "Where've you been? Do you know where Ben is? Janie was asking."

Maggie's gaze flew to the left side table near the front of the room. One peach-colored head, one white one and one bald one. She'd heard Charlie laughing last night telling someone that that circle of skin on top wasn't a bald spot, it was a solar panel for a raging love machine.

No Ben. Speaking of raging love machines. Maybe he'd tossed his things into his pickup and fled, leaving Janie and all the other grandmothers to fend for themselves. A clear case of committal-phobia. She tried to think of all the advice she'd ladled out for her readers about men who were afraid to commit, but failed to come up with a single piece of wisdom other than that some men—maybe even most men—were.

Opening her watercolor pad, she stared at the blank page and tried to remember if she'd said anything that would lead him to believe she expected anything of him. She didn't, not really. Not to say she wouldn't have considered some sort of a relationship, but not every relationship had to end in marriage. That was foolish idealism, and while she had her ideals, she was nobody's fool.

Somehow she managed to get through the class without attracting any further attention. Suzy was doodling on the back of a horrible watercolor. Janie waved at her, but didn't come over. Charlie looked at her, smiled, turned away and then turned back to look some more.

Merciful Heaven, did it show? Men talked...

Of course women talked, too, but Maggie would curl up and die if she thought anyone knew where she'd been for the past hour, much less what she'd been doing. For two cents she'd throw everything in the car and go home, mission unaccomplished.

When the session ended she headed for the shelter of the side porch. And wouldn't you just know it? Ben had beat her there. He was staring out at the distinctive profile of Pilot Knob, barely visible in the distance. Before she could sneak away he said, "I guess we'd better talk."

"Um…not really. I mean, I don't have anything on my mind." She waited, scarcely breathing, then added, "Do you?"

He blinked. Was that confusion she saw on his face? Surely not. Hunter was the kind of man who never put a foot wrong, literally or figuratively.

"Oh, well…I guess we do need to talk about the forgery." Maggie the magnanimous.

"Maggie, what happened—I don't want you to think—"

But before she could discover what it was he didn't want her to think, Charlie emerged from the house. "Now we're even out of beer!"

Saved by the bell. It was clear from his expression that Ben was thinking the same thing she was. "I could go get some," Maggie volunteered. "Make out a grocery list and I'll be glad to go." Forty-five minutes there, half an hour to shop, forty-five minutes back…that should allow her plenty of time to put what had happened into perspective. Getting over it was another thing altogether.

Ben said, "I'll do it. I need a few things, anyway."

"Add it to the list," Maggie said without meeting his eyes.

Ben thought, dammit, she had no intention of hearing him out. Not that he knew what he was going to say, but she couldn't just ignore what had happened. She wasn't that kind of a woman, that much he did know.

She huffed up a little bit, turned to go and caught her shoe on the door sill. Lunging away from the porch rail, he managed to catch her. "Easy there, you don't want to tear up the woodwork."

Her face turned pink and he thought she was going to slug him. Instead, she laughed. "Don't say it. I need to lose these shoes. Well, I hate to disillusion you but I can be just as clumsy barefooted." She looked pointedly at his slick-soled, slant-heeled boots. Shaking her head, she said, "You'll get yours, just wait."

"Hey, these are my good luck boots."

And then they both laughed, not that it was particularly funny, but as a relief valve, laughter served the purpose. Ben held on to her arm, but gently—not like he was trying to take control. Women like Maggie, he told himself, needed delicate handling. Needed someone to smooth the way before they charged out to save the world.

Charlie was in the kitchen scribbling on a strip of paper. Glancing up, he said, "Skim milk, too, but wait'll after the next session. Silver's brought down some mattes. He's going to show us how to crop out the bad parts."

Still a little self-conscious, Ben said, "Hey, as long as we're here, we might as well learn how to crop out the bad parts, right?"

"I think he means the bad parts of our paintings," Maggie said dryly.

"I knew that." He took the list Charlie gave him and tucked it into his pocket.

Both Suzy and Ann were at the table when Maggie slid into place a few minutes later. Other than looking tired, Ann looked perfectly healthy. "I heard Perry did the loosening up thing this morning," she said softly.

"You should've been here," Suzy said. "I thought for a minute I was back at the Fit'n Trim Gym. Bend, sweep to the left, sweep to the right, twenty reps and then stand up and do it all over again."

"He's a good teacher," the quiet brunette said. "He's been drawing and painting since he was in grade school. He actually did a year at Pratt and met some of the big name artists."

Suzy said dryly, "I toured the capitol once, but that doesn't make me a politician."

At the front of the room, Silver had placed one of his own watercolors on a standing easel. He held up a small matte, then moved it over first one section, then another. "What we're looking for is something that can be salvaged even if we have to sacrifice those parts that aren't working."

Maggie wondered which parts of this week she would salvage, given the chance.

"Think of it as mining for precious gemstones." Silver shifted the small horizontal matte to frame a log tobacco barn, a dead tree and part of a cornfield, blocking out the farmhouse that had been the center of interest.

She would salvage today. Wise or not, she would

salvage every single moment she spent with Ben Hunter.

Suzy said, "I still don't know exactly what he means by not working."

"Do you care?" Maggie whispered back.

"You have a question, Miss Riley?"

Well, heck. She might as well get something out of this blasted class after all the money she'd wasted on it. Mary Rose would just have to take her word for what a creep the man was, because so far Maggie hadn't come up with a scrap of proof in spite of Suzy's efforts. "I said I'm not sure what you mean by not working."

"Come closer, dear, perhaps it's your eyes that aren't working."

Or her brain, Maggie admitted ruefully. The implication was clear, and not all that unfounded.

Over the next several minutes the class was treated to a demonstration of how elements as small as a speck of bright color or a broken cornstalk pointing the wrong way could lead the eye out of the picture plane. It never occurred to Maggie to ask what a picture plane was. She really didn't care.

While Perry droned on and on about muddy colors and paint quality—about the difference between planned bleeds and unplanned blotches—Maggie wondered where Ben was. He hadn't joined the class. She listened for the sound of a vehicle leaving the parking lot, but all she heard was the rumble of distant thunder.

By the time Silver relented, her head was reeling with useless knowledge, her feet were killing her and all she could think of was that Ben had made love to her and she was probably doomed to spinsterhood. No other man could ever come up to his standard. It had nothing whatsoever to do with technique, but with the man himself. Whatever it was—chemical, biological or something more mystical—she was stuck with it.

She was packing up her material with some vague idea of leaving for good when Perry Silver's mellifluous voice rang out again. "There's a truism among artists. When the general public likes your work, you're in trouble. Do you know what I say?" He looked expectantly at his disciples. "Faugh on that. Perry says, faugh, faugh, faugh!"

Faugh? Now there was a word for you, Maggie thought, amused. This entire week, she had to admit, had been a learning experience. A few of the lessons she could have done without.

"I paint for the masses," the instructor announced, "not for the elite. If the general public appreciates my work, I know I've succeeded."

Then he'd obviously succeeded, scam or no scam. She'd heard nothing but raves from most of his students, several of whom would probably part with enough money to buy whatever he was selling.

Finally the last class of the day ended. The last as far as Maggie was concerned, at any rate. Tonight's session she would skip, if she were still here. For all the progress she was making, either as a painter or a sleuth, she might as well pack up and go home.

Ben was waiting for her when she emerged from her room a few minutes later. Without a word spoken on either side, he steered her to the front door. And like the dumbest lamb in the flock, she went.

The western sky had blackened, creating a dramatic backdrop for the narrow streak of late sunlight that gilded the treetops. Instead of lingering to appreciate the view, he nodded toward the arbor on the edge of the clearing.

Maggie was suddenly reluctant. She'd heard of butterflies in the belly. Hers tended to go for the brain. If he wanted to act as if today had never happened, two could play that game. Affecting an offhand manner, she said, "Maybe we're doing the man an injustice, did you ever think of that?"

"Who, Silver? Yeah, I thought about it. According to Janie, the guy really does know his stuff. He's won a whole bunch of awards in the state and local arena. The only thing I have a problem with is selling reproductions and claiming they're a great investment."

Pausing to finger a pebble from her sandal, Maggie steadied herself by clinging to his arm. Straightening, she said, "Okay, so maybe he's the next best thing to whatsisname, that guy who paints the four-eyed, dissected ladies. Maybe he's even made a fortune selling his stuff—and I'm sorry about your grandmother, I really am—but that doesn't mean he's in love with Mary Rose and not her trust fund."

"So what are you saying? There's no such thing as love at first sight?"

Her heart shifted into overdrive. "Pure urban myth," she said breathlessly.

"Okay, then what about this one? When it comes to love, rich women don't stand a chance."

Halting, she turned to face him and then wished she hadn't. It was almost impossible to think clearly when she was this close. Her hormones had taken over earlier today. Now it was time for the gray cells to step forward. "All I'm saying is that if Perry made as much money on art as the Dilyses have on pickles, there's a slight chance he truly loves her for herself. I really, really hope that's the case, honestly, I do. But I don't think so."

Ben's eyes narrowed. "Has he come on to you?"

"Do I look rich? Of course he hasn't, but I asked Suzy to—to sort of flirt with him, drop a few hints about her family's business."

"The hell with that, has he made a move toward you?"

Maggie looked at him as if he'd lost his wits. "For Pete's sake, why would he go after me when he could have someone like Suzy—or even Ann?"

He shook his head slowly. "You still don't get it, do you?"

"Sure I get it. Whenever I want it." And then, hearing what she'd just said, Maggie slapped a hand over her mouth, inwardly cursing her tendency to resort to glibness when she was nervous. "I mean, I can get a date any time I want one, but that's not why I'm here. Oh, shoot!" She closed her eyes. "You get me so mixed up!"

A slow grin spread over his face. "Good. I'll take any advantage I can get."

"Oh, no you won't."

"We need to talk about that, too, but let's get this other stuff out of the way first. How old is this friend of yours?" They had stopped a dozen feet away from the arbor.

"I already told you, she's twenty-five. A *young*

twenty-five.'' She tapped her foot, daring him to challenge her. If he thought she was making too much of her own maturity, he didn't mention it. Just as well. She could still clobber him.

Mature. Right.

''Any reason she can't think for herself?'' His tone was suspiciously reasonable.

''Other than the fact that her father's always treated her like a hothouse rose, I can't think of any. I keep telling her she needs to move into a place of her own, but she's afraid of hurting her folks' feelings.''

Ben did something with his mouth that was both maddening and provocative. She knew what that mouth could do, dammit. She didn't need to be reminded. ''Tell me something,'' he said. ''Do you still live at home?''

''That's different.''

''I expect it is,'' was all he said. With an arm at her back, he steered her toward the vine-covered arbor. If she had a grain of sense she'd turn around right now and go back inside. Any talking they did needed to be done in plain view of anyone who cared to look. There was safety in numbers.

''I've known her forever.'' Maggie had this habit of filling any uncomfortable silence with words, whether or not they were relevant. ''When we were little we used to play together. My dad does all Mr. Dilys's insurance, did I tell you that?''

His arms moved to her shoulder as he led her over a patch of rocky terrain. She could smell his pine-scented soap. When she'd stripped off her clothes earlier, she had smelled something earthy and green.

Never would she be able to look at moss in the same way.

Rather than break away and run back to the house—her first impulse—she focused on not tripping and tried to ignore the feel of him, the scent of him, and how comfortable the weight of his arm felt on her shoulder. She wanted desperately for him to approve of her, which was a bad sign. An incredibly bad sign, because for the most part, Maggie didn't give a hoot what anyone thought of her. Her father called her heedless, and she had to admit that the trait occasionally landed her in trouble.

"What a pair you must have made," Ben mused. They were only a few yards away from the shadowy arbor, with its cozy two-person swing.

"We still do. She writes letters to my column under an assumed name when things are slow so it looks like I've got this huge readership, and I take her to places she's never heard of and introduce her to some really neat people."

Ben shook his head. "I'd like to meet a few of what you call 'neat people.' Sometimes a woman can fall in with the wrong crowd and find herself in more trouble than she bargained for. You ever think about that?"

"All the time. For instance—"

But before she could get to her "for instance," they arrived at the arbor and stopped dead. Ben said, "Charlie, what are you doing out here?"

Someone laughed, a soft, husky sound that identified her even before the peach colored hair came into view.

"'Scuse us," Ben said, and backed away. As they

turned toward the house again, Maggie told herself she wasn't disappointed, not really. If she had a single grain of sense—which at the moment, was debatable—she'd call it a lucky reprieve.

Ben chuckled and Maggie said, "Maybe we could make reservations. For the arbor, I mean."

Kick yourself, woman!

"Good idea. I've got an even better one. How about we head for town, pick up whatever groceries are on the list and have dinner while we're out?"

Spending time alone together was like waltzing through a minefield. Maggie knew it. She had a feeling Ben knew it, too, unless today had meant no more to him than scratching a temporary itch.

Ten

The rain began in earnest before they were even halfway to town. With the windshield wipers and headlights on, Maggie leaned forward to switch on the defogger. Neither of them had brought any rain gear, but Ben said, "Miss Emma made me bring an umbrella. Told her I never used 'em, but she insisted."

"That's what grandmothers are for. Where is it?"

"Somewhere back there under a ton of junk." He nodded to the narrow space behind the driver's seat. "Rain'll be over by the time we get to town, anyway."

Before they'd set out he had glanced at a map, even though Maggie told him she knew the way. With rain coming down in curtains, maps were little help as they could barely see the road, much less the exit signs.

"Real frog strangler."

"Try for something more original. How about an ark floater? Ben, slow down," Maggie cautioned.

He slowed, but not too much. He didn't want to rear-end another vehicle, but neither did he want to slow up enough to risk being a road hazard. There was no sign of any taillights ahead, but that didn't mean they were the only ones on the highway. There were always a few nuts who thought that as long as they could see they didn't need lights.

Clutching her shoulder belt, Maggie leaned forward, peering through the wall of gray. "There ought to be an exit somewhere along here where we could—"

"Sit back. If I have to stop suddenly I don't want you—" He swore under his breath. "Sunovabitch!" Jerking the wheel sharply, he milked the brakes to a standstill within inches of a white van that had pulled off onto the shoulder at an angle, one corner projecting a few feet onto the highway.

Ben backed up a few feet, then steered cautiously onto the narrow shoulder, making sure he was completely off the highway. Maggie said, "I don't want to be here."

"Me, either." He waited a moment, then checked carefully for any sign of traffic before pulling out again. "Is there an overpass anywhere around here?"

She shook her head. "I don't think so. Anyway, it might not be wide enough if you were thinking about parking there until the rain slacked off."

"Yeah, you're probably right. Watch for an exit. We'd better find a place to wait it out."

* * *

The Laurel Lane Lodge looked as if it had survived the past half century unchanged. Of the five separate units, none appeared to be occupied, but there was a light on in the office.

"Sit tight." Ben ducked out and made a dash to the door.

The apron-clad woman behind the desk rose to meet him. "My mercy, would you look at this rain. Sauer's Branch is already up over the banks, I heard it on the radio. There's so much static you can't hardly hear anything. You need a place to stay?"

A few minutes later Ben slid into the truck again, soaked to the skin, but grinning. Brandishing a key, he said, "Any old port in a storm." His voice was barely audible over the sound of rain hammering down on the metal cab.

Maggie tried to pretend her pulse rate hadn't shot into the stratosphere. "If you wanted to show off your Texas roots, a broad-brimmed hat would've served a lot better than those boots."

"I'll match my boots against those things you're wearing any day. We drew number five, over there on the end." Inching along the short driveway, he pulled up in front of a small unit distinguished by a blue door and a single blue-shuttered window. "Stay here while I unlock."

Watching him dash toward the minuscule shelter, Maggie thought of all the motel jokes she'd ever heard. Under the circumstances, stopping was only sensible. It didn't necessarily mean they were going to dive into bed together. They could dry off and talk until the rain slacked off. Actually, it would be a good opportunity to get better acquainted—sharing childhood experiences, comparing notes on the progress of their individual missions. That should take all of two minutes. *Then* what?

As if she didn't know.

Deliberately she pushed away the thought that in a few days, once the workshop ended, they would each go their separate ways. Not that they would be all that far apart—not as long as he stayed with his grandmother. She hadn't asked about his future plans because first of all, it was none of her business. Now she was afraid to—afraid his plans didn't include her.

After only a short dash to the blue door they were both wet, thanks partly to the solid wall of water pouring off the roof. Maggie wouldn't have been surprised to see steam rising from Ben's shirt, the way it was plastered to his skin. His boots made a squeaky sound with every step. "Hope there's enough towels," he said, reaching the minuscule bathroom in three strides.

Self-conscious, Maggie studied the room that was dominated by a chenille-covered bed. Instead of the usual commercial carpet there were several scatter rugs on a varnished wood floor. "This reminds me of one of the illustrations in this book I used to have," she said, refusing to be intimidated by a bed. "I'm not sure if it was *Goldilocks* or *Little Red Riding Hood.*"

"Easy to tell the difference." Ben dropped a towel over her hair and gave it a few gentle rubs. "Depends on whether there's a wolf or a bear in the bed."

So then of course they both stared at the bed, which suddenly seemed to grow until there was nothing else in the room. Ben cleared his throat. He seemed almost as tense as she was. Moving abruptly, he crossed to the window, discovered that it wouldn't open, and opened the front door a crack. "Air's musty in here," he said gruffly. "Rain's not blowing from this direction.

He began unbuttoning his shirt and Maggie thought, not like this...please. It's too soon. She looked everywhere but at the man who absorbed all the oxygen in the small room. "You know what? I think this furniture is the real thing," she said brightly. "I mean genuine wood." Swallowing hard, she walked over and touched the leaf of a potted plant. "This is real, too. Real dirt and everything."

Marvelous, Maggie. Why not impress him with your brilliant conversational skills?

"Watch your step on these rugs, they're trippers," Ben cautioned. His shirt unbuttoned, he tugged it out of his pants. Before she could inform him that she didn't need a caretaker, he said, "Maggie, get out of those damp clothes before you start sneezing."

She wilted. All right, so he was bossy. It was the kindness in his voice that got to her. He wasn't just interested in getting her naked so he could have his way with her—not that his way wasn't hers, too.

"Oh, for Pete's sake," she muttered, turning away just as he peeled off his wet shirt.

Unfortunately, she turned toward the oval dresser mirror, and there he was again. Closing her eyes didn't help. They could be stranded together in a pitch-black cave and she would still be aware of him with every cell in her body. It had to be chemical. That pheromone thing, probably. She knew men who were handsomer—even a few who were built as well, but not a single one of them moved her at all. Somewhere inside her was an intricate lock, just waiting for the right key. And Ben Hunter was that key.

All right, she told herself—you're both adults. You've done it before, so what does it matter if you do it again? Where's the problem?

The problem was that she wanted more than sex.

"Maggie? You're frowning."

He appeared behind her in the mirror, his wide shoulders framing her narrower ones like a hawk hovering over a scared rabbit. "No'm not," she said, and forced a smile to prove it.

His hands closed over her shoulders. "Maggie, Maggie," he said with exaggerated patience. "Look, if you don't want to stay here we don't have to. We can wait in the truck for the rain to slack and head back. I know I promised you dinner, but it might have to wait."

"I'm fine. I mean this is only sensible. I mean, what if one of us had to go to the…" Chagrined, she closed her eyes. "Shut up, Maggie, just shut up."

Ben chuckled. "Take off your damp clothes. I can turn on the fan and they'll dry in no time."

They wouldn't, and they both knew it. Maggie might tell a white lie or two to spare someone's feelings, but she tried never to lie to herself. She had wanted this man almost from the first moment she'd seen him. Wanted him even before he'd kissed her. Out in the woods on a patch of moss beside a tiny waterfall, she had welcomed him into her arms, into her body. What had followed was a pleasure so profound she knew it would be with her 'til her dying day.

A realist, Maggie told herself that whatever happened now, it was an inevitable extension of what had happened earlier. It really didn't change anything.

"So," she said, her voice half an octave higher than usual. "Shall we...sit down? If we had a deck of cards..."

There wasn't a damned thing to do in here but go to bed. There wasn't even an old newspaper she could pretend to read. Nothing but the bed looming behind them.

Ben watched her in the mirror, trying to figure out what was going on under that shaggy mop of damp hair. He couldn't quite get a handle on Maggie Riley—possibly because she didn't play any of the games he'd come to expect from the women he took to bed.

She was nervous, which told him that despite what had happened earlier she didn't take this sort of thing for granted. As it couldn't be for lack of opportunity he could only conclude that few men had managed to break through her prickly defenses.

Still facing the mirror, he slipped his arms around her waist from behind. Under the clinging fabric of her dress, her small breasts were clearly visible, her nipples dark and alert. She closed her eyes as he began unfastening the row of pearl buttons. "Maggie?" he whispered, and she nodded.

He deliberately lingered over the task of undressing her, savoring each small step. Allowing the tension to build until it was all but irresistible. Her body might be slight, but there was no mistaking its maturity. Judging from the way she was pressing herself against his arousal, she was as eager as he was.

This woman won't be so easy to forget. Ignoring the soft, insistent whisper, he led her toward the bed. It was a double, not even a queen size. His inconvenient conscience urged him to issue the standard disclaimer to the effect that, despite what had happened earlier and what was about to happen now, there was nothing binding on either side.

But hell, she knew that. He didn't have to put it into words.

Turning her in his arms, he lowered his lips to hers. The fleeting thought crossed his mind as he deepened the kiss, savoring what was to come, that he could easily become addicted to this woman.

When she began tugging at his belt, he reached for the bottom of the silky undershirt thing she was wearing and eased it up under her arms. There was no way of getting it over her head without ending the kiss. Reluctantly, he lifted his head. Then, in an impromptu dance, she kicked off her sandals and wriggled the rest of the way out of her damp top.

Ben took a moment to appreciate the perfection of her, from her small, rounded thighs to her small rounded hips—to the waist he could practically span with his hands and the small, proud swell of her breasts.

Dropping his jeans around his knees, he attempted to step out of them and nearly tripped. He cursed under his breath, but managed to keep it brief and relatively clean.

"You might want to take off your boots first." Maggie's dry observation brought forth a snort of laughter that did nothing at all to reduce the tension.

"Yes, ma'am. Uh—how about closing the front

door.'' He'd forgotten they'd left it partly open to air out the room.

Naked but for a scrap of yellow silk that just missed being a thong, she lunged for the door, slammed it and fastened the chain. ''Oh, for gosh sakes, anyone passing by could've looked in!'' She switched off the overhead light but left on a forty-watt lamp on the dresser.

Ben shucked off his boots and socks, then peeled off his jeans and briefs in one swift motion. Glancing up, he said, ''Watch that rug.''

She wrinkled her nose at him. ''You know me too well.''

''Yeah, I do,'' he said, realizing it was no less than the truth.

With one knee on the edge of the mattress, she hesitated. ''Um—do you—that is—''

''I do,'' he said, and held up a foil packet.

''Good, because I don't, and we didn't earlier this afternoon.'' She said it in a half-joking way, trying to sound as if she did this sort of thing all the time.

Ben knew better. He really did know Maggie Riley, no matter if they had met only a few days ago. ''Come here,'' he said, his voice a rough caress.

There was none of the awkwardness that some-times occurred between new lovers. Even the first time, there had been no real awkwardness, only ea-gerness—only a sense of inevitability.

Now, starting with another hungry kiss, they picked up where they had left off and quickly moved beyond. All senses alive, Ben felt the satiny heat of her skin— he breathed in the intoxicating scent of fruity sham-poo and warm, aroused woman and heard the tiny whimpering sounds, the soft gasps she made as he explored her slender perfection. Her nipples were ripe cherries begging to be plucked. He plucked them, first with his fingertips, then with his lips and teeth.

Gasping, she ran her hands over his chest, raking his flat nipples until they stood up like small cartridges.

"Honey, maybe we'd better slow down," he said even as his hands made forays under the sheet that brought forth another shuddering gasp. *Slow down? Man, are you crazy?*

No guarantees on that front.

Her fingers twisted the flat curls that crossed his chest before spearing down to his groin. At this rate he'd better suit up fast, or it would be too late. Amazing, the degree of pressure that could build up when a man went too long without sex, he told himself, unwilling to admit that it was the woman herself and not the long, dry spell that had ended only hours earlier.

"I don't want to slow down. Make love to me, Ben."

With her small hands probing dangerously close to ground zero, he whispered roughly, "Neither do I." Using his teeth and his free hand, he ripped the corner off the foil packet he'd had the forethought to put within reach.

"Sweet—creamery—butter," he whispered roughly as he first gloved himself in protection and then in her warm, welcoming body. "Maggie, I don't want to rush you, but—"

"You're not." She was moving restlessly, each shuddering breath clearly audible. Her hands fluttered over whatever parts of him they could reach, igniting small brushfires along the way.

He pulled back, looming over her, his face tense with urgency. When she protested, he rolled over onto his back, carrying her with him so that she bracketed his hips with her thighs. He probably outweighed her by a good seventy-five pounds. He should have thought of that out by the waterfall, but he hadn't been thinking at all—at least not with his brain.

"Go, girl," he directed, his voice so strained as to be unrecognizable.

She needed no prompting. Lifting her hips, she centered herself and settled down again with such exquisite slowness he died several deaths before he could even remember to breathe. Steeling himself against snatching control and racing for the finish line, he let her move at her own pace, every muscle in his body quivering with tension.

Her pace started out slow and easy, but then, as if she'd lost the rhythm and couldn't get back in step, it became jerky and fast. She started to whimper. Clasping her shoulders, Ben melded his pace to hers until suddenly she ground herself hard against him, her eyes widening.

"Oh, oh, oh!" The soft sound of discovery cascaded over him like a benediction.

He held her tightly in place as a million volts of pure energy shot through him, echoing repeatedly throughout every cell of his body.

Eventually she collapsed, damp and panting. "Oh, my goodness," she whispered breathlessly.

"Yeah," he said as blood began to filter back to his brain. "My thoughts precisely."

                              *   *   *

The sky had mostly cleared by the time they ventured outside. Tufts of pink-edged clouds drifting overhead as traffic appeared to be running normally again, tires singing on wet pavement. The small parking area outside their cottage was littered with puddles and leaves from newly green trees.

"I'm hungry," Maggie said, a note of surprise in her voice. "Do we still have time to get something to eat?" There was none of the awkwardness she might have expected.

"You operating on a deadline?" Ben opened the passenger side door and helped her up. Her legs were short, the 4x4 was high, the running board little more than a narrow chrome bar. It occurred to him that he really didn't need four-wheel drive any longer.

The thought was followed by a shaft of unease. Just because a man had sex with a woman a few times, that was no cause to start changing his lifestyle. Maggie sure as hell wasn't making an issue of it. Some women wanted to talk afterward. All he'd ever wanted to do was sleep, preferably alone.

Not that he'd have minded talking to Maggie, but she'd clammed up tighter than a tick on a shorthaired dog and headed for the shower. Then, while she'd dressed, he had showered. There hadn't been a whole lot of opportunity for conversation.

"Barbecue all right with you?" he asked casually as they turned off highway 52 toward Pilot Mountain. There was a sign ahead that promised Lexington-style barbecue, which meant lean pork in a light, tomato-based sauce. It took some getting used to after the heavy-bodied beef 'que he was used to, but it wasn't bad. Not half-bad, in fact.

"Love it," she said brightly. A little too brightly, he suspected, but then he wasn't quite as relaxed as he was making out to be, either.

She sighed and continued to watch the scenery go by while he drove and tried not to think of either the immediate past or the future.

Neither of them did justice to the barbecue. Maggie nibbled on a sweet, greasy hushpuppy while Ben looked around for some hot sauce and used it liberally on his mild, eastern style sandwich. He said, "You put slaw on yours?"

She said, "You're supposed to."

"Not where I come from."

"So?"

And that settled that. East was east and west was west, and all the rest of it.

Outside a small independent grocery store a few minutes later, Maggie glanced over the list. Ben insisted on giving her a fifty-dollar bill and offered to help shop.

"Since I'm not used to help it would be more of a hindrance, but thanks."

He was waiting outside the truck when she emerged with a grocery cart. Together they crammed the bags onto the back seat. Neither of them spoke more than a few words on the drive back to Peddler's Knob as for once, Maggie found herself incapable of filling in an awkward silence with mindless chatter.

Only when they pulled into the parking lot did she speak. Unclipping her seat belt, she peered up at the house. "It looks like every light in the house is on. I wonder why."

"Because it's dark outside? Come on, I'll get Charlie to help bring in the supplies."

When they reached the steps, slick from the recent rain, he took her hand. Rather than make an issue of it, Maggie let him guide her up onto the porch. Was there a tactful way of letting him know she didn't expect anything from him? In case one of her readers ever asked her about the protocol for afternoon sex by a waterfall or evening sex in a rented room, she would have to refer them to Dr. Ruth or Dr. Laura. Miss Maggie hadn't a clue.

She slanted a sidelong glance at the man beside her and saw that he was frowning. She wanted to say, "Look, so we went to bed together a couple of times. We're consenting adults, a good time was had by all, and that's the end of that, period."

Only it wasn't. Not for her, at least. So she didn't say it.

Charlie met them at the door. "Where the hell have you two been? Are you both feeling all right?"

Maggie darted another look at Ben, wondering if it showed. Had she buttoned her dress wrong?

Ben said, "We got caught in a cloudburst, that's all. What's going on?"

"You didn't eat supper?"

Ben nodded and Maggie said, "We had barbecue. We could have brought some back if we'd thought of it. The supplies are—"

Charlie said, "Heck with that, long's you didn't eat here. They're dropping like flies. Janie and Georgia and I did the cooking tonight, but it wasn't that, I swear."

Eleven

Thank goodness she'd showered at the motel before they'd left, Maggie told herself, because the ladies' bathroom was not a particularly pleasant place. Three people so far had come down with symptoms of food poisoning. Two more were looking iffy.

Janie said, "I called a doctor. He said bring 'em in, but I don't know…"

"Pity they don't make house calls anymore," said a brisk, white-haired woman named Bea who was cooking rice. Seeing Maggie staring at the pot on the stove, she said, "It'll help some. Cola's for them that can keep it down. With all this rain, the saltines are limp as raw bacon."

Maggie said, "Oven. Crisp 'em in the oven." Good Lord, what was going on around here? She'd left an art workshop and come back to find a field hospital.

Janie stood in the middle of the kitchen and waved a cooking spoon. "Attention, everyone. I'll coordinate for the duration, all right? Charlie, you see that there's a bucket beside every bed. Round up the water containers from the studio. You, Maggie—and you, Ben—go up to the third floor and see where Perry's hiding out. He hasn't been downstairs since all this started."

"Probably on the phone with his lawyer right this minute," said Georgia.

Following Ben up to the second floor, Maggie couldn't believe that little more than an hour ago she'd been lying in his arms, trying not to think about wedding bells—about riding off into the sunset on a white horse with the cowboy of her choice.

Actually, she was a lot smarter than that, only sometimes her imagination got in the way of her common sense. Despite his boots and his accent, Ben wasn't John Wayne, she reminded herself. What he was, was an unemployed Texan who happened to be visiting a relative, who happened to live in North Carolina.

Moans, groans and more ominous sounds greeted them as they hurried along the second floor hall to the attic stairway. The door was always kept closed. For all she knew, it might even be locked.

It wasn't. "Maybe you'd better let me go up alone," Ben said.

"No way. You might need backup."

"Maggie—" He shook his head, opened the door and set off up the narrow, steep steps, with Maggie two steps behind him. The only light showing was a dim glow coming from the far end of a long, slope-ceiling room. It was the light they'd seen from the parking lot.

Two steps from the top, he paused. To steady herself, Maggie looped her fingers under his belt and tried to peer around him through the clutter of boxes, stacks of empty frames and what looked like a small guillotine. As there was no blood, only a few scraps of matte board under the wicked blade, Maggie managed to control her alarm.

Ann was seated at a desk at the far end. She glanced up and her eyes widened. "What are you two doing up here?"

Ben had to bend to avoid bumping his head. "Watch it," he warned as Maggie followed close on his heels.

"One good thing about being height challenged," she whispered. "I'm good with low clearances." And then she said, "Why am I whispering? Ann, are you all right? You do know what's going on downstairs, don't you?"

Ann held a finger over her lips, casting her eyes toward a door that had been hidden until now. "Shh, Perry doesn't feel good. He's trying to get a nap before he heads back to town."

Avoiding the eaves, Ben dodged the cartons and stacks. "If he's got the same symptoms as everybody else, he'll be better off on the second floor —that is, unless there's a john up here."

Ann's frown was replaced by a look of concern. "Symptoms?"

"Food poisoning," Maggie supplied.

Ann sat down again. "You're kidding. I thought it

was just his wrist. He takes all this herbal stuff and sometimes it makes him feel, you know—yukky.''

"Did either of you eat here tonight?" Ben asked.

Maggie was distracted by the label on several of the boxes. Good heavens, Hong Kong again? She was pretty sure Perry had said his three-hundred-pound watercolor paper was French, not Chinese.

"I haven't had time to eat since breakfast. Perry's been in his room since the late session. He stays over sometimes, but he's got an apartment in town."

"Did either of you go down for supper?"

Ann shook her head slowly. "I made a sandwich and brought it up with me while I was…" She glanced at the cluttered desk and looked away.

"Where is he, through here?" Ben was halfway to the inconspicuous door when Ann blocked his way.

"Let me," she said. "I'm pretty sure he's okay, but like I said, he takes all this herbal stuff. I doubt if any of it's ever been FDA approved, but you know Perry—you can't tell him anything."

Maggie moved slowly around the angular room, eyeing the stack of prints—reproductions or whatever they were called. Still with her hand on the doorknob, Ann said, "He's got that carpal tunnel thing now, but the truth is, he's always had some excuse to keep from doing whatever he doesn't want to do. He's my cousin on my mama's side, so I've tried to help— you know how it is with family—but honestly, there's times lately when I feel like telling him…"

Shaking her head, she quietly opened the door. "Perry? Are you awake?"

It was a subdued group that met in the kitchen later that night. The worst of the sickness was evidently over. "They'll live," said Charlie, "but they're feeling pretty drained."

Groans could be heard around the table, where an array of safe snacks had been set out. Charlie, who hadn't been affected, said, "Sorry. No pun intended. Stuff acts like salmonella. I figure it had to be either the raw cider or the sprouts. Not everybody put sprouts on their salad, and not everybody drank the cider, but I tossed the leftovers just in case."

"Godalmighty." After emptying pails for the past few hours Ben was too tired to watch his language. The brow-soothing and hand-holding had been left to Janie, Georgia and Maggie, while the woman called Bea had manned the kitchen, brewing tea, serving up warm ginger ale and oven-crisped saltines

"How's Perry doing? Is Ann looking after him?" Bea asked.

"Evidently his stomach's fine," Maggie told her. "It's his carpal tunnel that's acting up."

"Just in time to keep him from being pressed into service in the bucket brigade," Ben commented.

Charlie slathered mustard on a corned beef sandwich. Evidently his appetite hadn't been affected. "Carpal tunnel? Must come from painting all those thousands of picket fences and dead twigs."

"That's what Ann says anyway, and she's known him all her life. They're cousins."

Nobody seemed to know what to say after that. Georgia twisted her wedding rings. Janie handed Charlie a paper napkin when his sandwich dripped mustard on his shirt, and Ben wheeled his chair around, stretched his long legs in front of him and sighed. "What now? We break camp, shut down and go home?"

"He can still talk. He doesn't have to use his wrist to teach," Georgia offered.

Maggie leaned forward, arms crossed on the long wooden table. She didn't want to go home. They were all exhausted, but if they packed up and left, where would Ben go? To his grandmother's house? Back to Texas? She felt like crying, and not only because it was late and she was bone tired.

"I left something in the truck," he said softly. They'd brought in the supplies earlier. "Maggie, how about a short walk to help you sleep?"

"I don't need a walk, thanks. I don't even need to be horizontal, all I need is to let my eyes close." Her lids were already drooping, but she got up and followed him to the door. Dead and in her grave she would probably follow him if he so much as crooked his little finger.

As Perry was fond of saying, Faugh!

Once outside, Ben told her he'd be leaving the next day. "First thing tomorrow, matter of fact." He eyed her uncertainly. When she didn't react, he said, "So I was just wondering...will you be all right?"

Stunned, she took only a moment to recover. "I think I'll stay on for the last couple of days. I'm really getting into this—this art stuff." It was a lie and they both knew it, but it was the best she could do on short notice.

"Maggie? You're sure you're okay?"

What had he expected her to do, throw herself in his arms and beg him never to leave her? She might look like a weakling on the outside, but inside she was tough as nails. "I'm sorry about your grand-mother, but at least maybe she'll enjoy her prints—reproductions—whatever."

Ben nodded. It wasn't Miss Emma's so-called prints he wanted to talk about. He'd already made up his mind to buy them from her, offering her twice what she'd paid. It would just about wipe out his bank account, but what the heck. He could tell her he knew of a man back in Texas who'd be glad to take them off his hands.

He would deal with Miss Emma tomorrow. Right now he had another problem that would never have become a problem if he hadn't suffered a major lapse in judgment. "Maggie, I have to go back to Dry Creek for a few days—maybe even a few weeks—but—"

"That's great! I mean, you must be getting home-sick. I know I would be if I had to—well, anyway, just drive safe, all right?"

He'd be flying, not driving. Not that he bothered to correct her. Before she turned away he saw a sus-picion of tears in her eyes.

Sweet Jesus, he didn't want to hurt this woman, but if he told her why he had to leave, he'd have to tell her the whole ugly story. He'd just as soon not leave her with that impression. Until he dealt with the past, though, he couldn't afford to think about the future.

"It's been a long day," she said with quiet dignity, and he watched her walk back to the shabby old man-sion. She stumbled only once on the steep, graveled path.

"Damned shoes," he swore softly. She wasn't

fooling anyone, and he had a feeling she knew it. Maggie wasn't a pretender. She was a straight-shooter. She expected the same of the people she let herself get close to, and God knows, they'd been close. So close it was threatening to undermine everything he'd always taken for granted. Such as being married to a cop was a high-risk position for any woman.

He waited until she was inside, then he called on his cell phone and booked his flight. Packing wouldn't take long. He had a few more goodbyes to say, but those would wait until morning. Whereas with Maggie...

Had she believed him when he said he'd be back? Had he believed himself?

"Damn Ben Hunter, anyway." Maggie stumbled over the sandals she'd just kicked off. Why couldn't he have had the decency to ignore her? So what if she'd been attracted to him? What woman with a viable hormone wouldn't be? She should have known better than to sleep with him though, especially after dealing with the very same kind of heartbreak practically every week in her column.

Although admittedly, some of the letters were from Mary Rose.

And that was another thing, she thought as she rummaged through her suitcase for some of the snack foods she'd brought with her. Angrily, she bit into a Moon Pie, scattering crumbs down her nonexistent bosom. All things considered, this whole week had been a waste of time. She should have stayed home where at the very least she could have seen that her father ate decent meals and didn't smoke more than the one cigar a day his doctor allowed him.

After a largely sleepless night, Maggie had been tempted to throw her things into her car and take off, but sheer stubbornness prevailed. If she left first, Ben would know why, and that she couldn't have borne. If he'd even greeted her this morning with a smile instead of a wary nod, she might have felt better, but he hadn't. She watched as he spoke to Charlie, to Bea and a few others, and hugged Janie and Georgia.

Not so much as a smile in Maggie's direction.

She stirred a third spoonful of sugar into her breakfast coffee. Fine. They'd said their goodbyes last night, nothing more to be said. She would damn well show a little class if it killed her.

And then Perry showed up in the kitchen. Was it only her imagination, or did he look a bit apprehensive? Probably spent the past few hours poring over the fine print in his liability policy.

Ben cornered him and the two men stepped out into the hall. Maggie strained to hear what was said, but others were talking and she caught only a few words. Ben was speaking quietly, but Perry's voice suddenly cut through the desultory conversation.

"Don't threaten me, dammit! What do you know about anything? You wouldn't know a giclee from a serigraph, you're nothing but a— a security guard!"

Oh ho, she thought—this isn't about last night, after all. Way to go, Texas! She made up her mind on the spot to write a column exposing—

Exposing what? The truth was, she still didn't know enough about the subject to write about it.

Maybe she'd better stick to writing advice to the lovelorn. She definitely knew about being lovelorn, if "lorn" meant being depressed, discouraged and angry all at the same time. If it meant wanting to kick something or throw something, or just curl up and cry until she ran out of tears.

A thin-lipped Perry marched into the studio and slammed the door. Maggie remained in the kitchen, ignoring her cooling cup of coffee. Ben collected the two small bags he'd set by the front door and headed out to his truck.

Maggie watched from the house, her throat aching the way it did just before the hurt spilled over into tears. At least one of them had accomplished something. From now on Perry might not be so quick to offer his pretty pictures as investments. Personally, she couldn't tell the difference between a zircon and a diamond, but if she ever needed money in a hurry, a zircon wouldn't do her much good.

As for Mary Rose, she might just have to learn her lesson the hard way. Any rescuing Maggie did from now on would be strictly through her column.

Halfway to the parking lot she saw Ben drop his bags and turn back toward the house. Without even thinking, she headed outside, across the porch and down the steps.

They met halfway. For one long moment they simply looked at each other. Ben said, "I'll call you."

No you won't, Maggie thought. But she nodded, unable to think of a single thing to say that wouldn't betray her true feelings.

"Maggie, about yesterday..."

The worst actress in the world, she tipped back her

head and laughed. "You mean the food poisoning? What a mess! Thank goodness we ate in town."

Through the studio windows they could hear Perry speaking in triplicate again. Something about "Values, values, values!"

"Write down your phone number for me," he said. "Got a pencil?" She shook her head, so he patted his pockets down and came up with a stubby drawing pencil. "Here's my number. I always have my cell phone with me." He handed her the scrap of paper—a gas station receipt.

"I rarely carry mine," she said, just to be contrary. If she thought he might actually call her, she would sleep with the thing. Bathe with it. But she told him her number and he wrote that down on a card from his billfold.

In whisky-clear eyes, she should have been able to read all sorts of hidden messages. The books always talked about things like that—how a woman could read a man's true thoughts in his eyes.

Maggie couldn't read a blessed thing, maybe because her own eyes were burning with unshed tears. She blurted the first thing she could think of. "You were right—about the forgery, I mean. Ann was signing his name on all those pictures because of his wrist."

Ben nodded.

"That makes it even worse, I guess. I mean..."

"I know what you mean, Maggie." It was as if they were both speaking a foreign language that bore no relation to what was in their minds. At least, none to what Maggie was thinking.

Ben turned to go, then reversed once more. When

he swept her into his arms, her feet actually left the ground. The kiss, as sweet as it was, held more than a touch of desperation. It ended far too quickly.

"Later," he said gruffly, and turned away once again. This time he didn't come back. Maggie watched him all the way to the pickup, watched him open the door and swing himself inside.

Long-legged men, she thought wistfully. Long, lean, strong, graceful—all the beautiful things a man could be. There ought to be a law against them. At the very least, the federal meat inspectors should stamp a warning in purple ink on their sides.

When his dust died away—there wasn't much of it on account of yesterday's rain—she went back inside and actually considered joining the class. Before she did anything else, though, she was going to retrieve her cell phone, in case he thought of something else he wanted to say.

"You're pathetic, you know that?" she muttered.

Just as she reached the room, she heard the quiet buzz of the cell phone she'd left on the dresser. Startled, she stopped dead for an instant, then she nearly broke her neck lunging across the room.

"Hello?" Oh, God, please let him have changed his mind about leaving.

She hadn't even bothered to check the numbers when she heard a familiar voice. "Maggie, where in the world have you been, I've been trying to call you since forever! You'll never guess what's happened!" There was a pause while Maggie tried to swallow her disappointment. And then, "Mag, it's me, Mary Rose. Say something!"

Without waiting, her friend rushed on. "Guess

what, I've lost seven pounds—I know, I know, it's mostly water weight so far, but my waistband's are getting loose, and I'm getting a really terrific tan. There's this new lotion—I'll tell you about it when I get home. Look, do you think you could make me an appointment with Zelle for a cut and maybe some color for two weeks from now? Because, wait'll you hear—I've met this really neat man…''

Two minutes later Maggie was still holding the tiny instrument in her hand, staring dumbly at the wall. ''She met this really neat man,'' she repeated softly. ''Well, shoot!''

All the way back to Miss Emma's neat frame house in Mocksville, Ben thought about his options and the situation he'd got himself involved in. He'd called his grandmother last night, letting her know he'd be stopping by before catching a late evening flight from Greensboro International.

Maybe he should have explained to Maggie why he had to leave, but then he'd have had to tell her about the ugly mess he'd left behind. Dammit all to hell and back, why couldn't someone else have uncovered the truth and turned over the evidence to I.A.? The thing that worried him most was that Mercy—the man who had saved his butt when he'd been a street-smart kid headed down a dead-end road—Mercy had gone along with it. Maybe he hadn't been involved personally, but he'd known. He had to have known. Hell, he'd admitted to just wanting to hang in there 'til he retired to secure his benefits package.

Ben knew he could've told Maggie simply that he

had to go back and testify in a court case, but that he'd be back as soon as the trial was over in case she wanted to pick up where they'd left off, but—

That's where he pulled up short. Even if Maggie was willing, how far down that particular road did he want to go? As far as he was concerned, it was unexplored territory. And while he wasn't a coward, he never liked to go into any situation unprepared.

How the hell did a man prepare for falling in love?

Twelve

Purely because she hated to admit defeat, Maggie stayed to the bitter end. She helped Ann matte the new shipment of reproductions—she called them that deliberately. Soon Ann was calling them that, too. Several would go on display at the end-of-the-workshop exhibit along with two of his originals.

Evidently Ben had spread the word before he left, because she heard Georgia telling one of the librarians that she intended to buy a copy of *Stone Mill in Winter* to hang over the bookcase in her dining room—because she liked it, not because she considered it an investment. Janie entered the conversations, and the print versus original thing was openly discussed.

Ann winked at Maggie and whispered, "I'm glad they know. I couldn't say anything because Aunt Iola, Perry's mama, lent my brother a down payment on his house, and Brother hasn't paid her back yet."

There would be other workshops, other exhibits, and probably other people talked into buying reproductions as an investment. Ben had done all he could, but Maggie hadn't. She still had a column to write.

Ben had left his paints behind, including all his awful attempts at landscape painting. Maggie matted what she considered his best attempt for the exhibit and put the rest of his gear with her own. After tonight's festive "opening" she would load her car and get an early start tomorrow.

The celebration was dismal. Not even the wine helped. Charlie claimed he never drank screw-top wines as they gave him headaches. He and Janie were openly holding hands now. Maggie warmed to the thought that they'd been able to put the past behind them and look forward to a new future.

Don't waste time, she wanted to urge. Follow your heart!

But then, who was she to advise anyone? Just because she wrote an advice column...

Faugh, as Perry would say.

The next morning she hugged them all goodbye, even those she hadn't got to know very well. Even Perry. For all his faults, he was probably a competent painter and an excellent teacher. Not that he'd been able to teach her to paint, but at least she knew now that being an artist involved a lot more than splashing paint on a blank piece of paper and calling it art.

Home was just as she'd left it. The lawn needed mowing, the gutters still needed cleaning and there was a sinkful of dirty dishes, despite the fact that they had a dishwasher. Sooner or later she would get around to everything.

Her father wasn't home yet, but then he often worked on Sundays when he could have the office to himself. Maggie checked his room, collected the clothes that needed laundering, stripped his bed and remade it after opening several windows to air out the cigar smoke.

Her own room was just as she'd left it, too. She set up the laptop computer she hadn't bothered to open back at Peddler's Knob, already thinking about the column she would write as soon as she got something cooking for supper.

Her mind still free-ranging over possibilities, she sorted through the mail to see if there was anything for Miss Maggie. Only a single letter from a man wanting to know if a wife was obligated to do all the housework even if she had an outside job.

That one she would definitely answer. She might even invent a few more letters along the same lines to get her point across. As long as both partners were working outside the home, she thought, mentally phrasing her response while she scrubbed sweet potatoes, wrapped them in foil, and shoved them in the oven, then both partners should share equally in household chores.

She was catching up on the news on television later that night when her cell phone buzzed softly from the kitchen where she'd left it. She hurried to answer it before it could wake her father, who had fallen asleep reading the *Journal*.

The minute she heard that familiar gravelly drawl

he stopped breathing. "Maggie? Are you there? Hello?"

"Ben," she exclaimed when she could finally harness her brain to her tongue. "Did you make it home all right? Well, of course you didn't—it's too soon. How long does it take to get there, anyway?"

She forced herself to relax and take a deep breath.

Ignoring her questions, he said, "I wanted to tell you when I'll be back."

"Back as in...?" Her heart knocked out an extra beat.

"Back as in North Carolina. As in a few miles from where you live."

Some five minutes later she punched off and laid her phone aside, still dazed. He was coming back. Not only to see his grandmother, who apparently had discovered eBay and was turning into something of an art dealer, but to see her—Maggie.

Ben had said Miss Emma was making only enough profit to cover the cost of shipping and insurance, but Maggie could tell how proud he was. Not that he'd ever said much about his family, but she had a feeling his early life had been vastly different from her own. Even after her mother had left, she'd had her father, two aunts, an uncle and half a dozen cousins. All Ben had was the woman he called Miss Emma.

"And me," she whispered. "He's coming back, he's coming back," she sang, clasping her arms around herself.

Don't get your hopes up too high, a small voice warned.

In the lounge chair across the living room, her father snored softly. Maggie wondered how he would get along if she left home and moved to Texas. Could she do it?

Too many questions, too few answers. Not even Miss Maggie could predict the future.

It was almost three weeks later when a familiar dark green pickup pulled into the driveway. Maggie was on a ladder dodging oak branches while she cleaned out the gutters. They hadn't been cleaned since last fall. Already small oak trees were sprouting there.

There were a thousand green trucks on the highway, she told herself. A million. Nevertheless, she nearly broke her neck scrambling down the ladder.

"Wait!" Ben yelled, jogging the last few steps. "Don't move!"

Halfway down she froze, but only for a moment. That was all the time it took for him to reach up and grab her around the waist and swing her down into his arms.

"God, I missed you," he said fervently. "Your shoestring's untied."

Ben had taken time only to stop by his grandmother's house, leave his bags and get directions to Maggie's house. Miss Emma said she had a bridge date that night, but she'd leave a casserole in the oven in case he made it back.

Food was the last thing on his mind.

"Ah, Maggie, Maggie, you'll never believe how much I missed you," he growled. Wrapped around him like a honeysuckle vine, her legs around his waist, her arms around his neck, she was either laughing or sobbing, he couldn't tell which. Didn't much care as long as she let him hold her.

"Put me down and kiss me," she ordered.

"The two are not mutually exclusive," he told her, and then he proved it.

A long time later, Maggie told him he might as well stay and meet her father, who had remained downtown for a Chamber of Commerce meeting.

"You need to meet Miss Emma, too. You'll like her. You two are a whole lot alike in some ways."

"Are you going to be here long?" The hesitancy in her voice made him ache.

"Like I told you, I've finished my business in Dry Creek. I'm ready to make a move." He'd ended up having only to give one more written deposition. Several other witnesses had been found and were ready to testify. Chief Mercer had cut a deal, so the case was pretty much in the bag.

It was a lousy ending to some good years in his life—the best years, so far. But he had a strong feeling that was about to change.

"And?" Maggie asked the leading question, sounding half-hopeful, half-fearful. He hadn't come right out and said the words, but she had to know how he felt. Hell, he was here, wasn't he? He'd left his truck in long-term parking at the airport in Greensboro, knowing he would be back. That was a testament to something, wasn't it?

Nearly an hour later, lying on his back with one arm around Maggie, the other propped under his head, Ben studied the smears of green, gray and purple that had been framed and hung where it could be seen from the bed. Frowning, he said, "That looks kind of familiar. Almost like…"

"Your last masterpiece? It is. The genuine thing, too, and not just a copy. Actually, it's kind of nice, once you stop thinking that it's supposed to look like something."

If Ben had been in any doubt about what love felt like, that was no longer the case. Lust would carry a man only so far. Love was what carried him the rest of the way.

"The best of both worlds," he murmured, burying his face in her hair.

"Is that the title?"

"Yeah," he said with a satisfied smile. "That's the title."

* * * * *

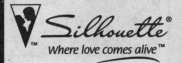

SPECIAL EDITION™

From *USA TODAY* bestselling author

SHERRYL WOODS

PRICELESS

(Silhouette Special Edition #1603)

Famed playboy Mick Carlton loved living
the fast life—with even faster women—
until he met Dr. Beth Browning.
Beth's reserved, quiet ways soon had him
wanting to believe in a slow and easy,
forever kind of love. Could Mack convince
Beth that his bachelor days were over?

**The second installment
in the popular miniseries**

MILLION DOLLAR DESTINIES

Three brothers discover all the riches money can't buy.

Available April 2004 at your favorite retail outlet.

COMING NEXT MONTH